"You're Lu[cky You Didn't] Lose [Your Life]"

Blue eyes snapped with anger and left no doubt of the owner's disdain for Julie Dever. But Julie couldn't understand why *he* was angry. It was *she* who had broken her collarbone.

"It's all your fault," she raged. "If your car lights hadn't blinded me, I wouldn't have swerved off the road. Now I have no money or a place to stay tonight."

A hint of amusement passed over Nicholas Raffer's lips. Swiftly and with ease he held Julie in his arms, pressing her against his unyielding chest.

"Well, *Ms.* Dever," he slowly drawled, "your problems are solved—for now. You're spending the night with me."

PARRIS AFTON BONDS, the bestselling historical romance author, lives in Dallas with her husband and children. This is her first Silhouette Romance.

Dear Reader,

Silhouette Romances is an exciting new publishing series, dedicated to bringing you the very best in contemporary romantic fiction from the very finest writers. Our stories and our heroines will give you all you want from romantic fiction.

Also, *you* play an important part in our future plans for Silhouette Romances. We welcome any suggestions or comments on our books, which should be sent to the address below.

So enjoy this book and all the wonderful romances from Silhouette. They're for *you!*

Silhouette Books
Editorial Office
47 Bedford Square
LONDON
WC1B 3DP

PARRIS AFTON BONDS
Made for Each Other

Silhouette Romance
Published by Silhouette Books

For Kit O'Brien Jones - a true Southern gentlewoman.

Copyright © 1981 by Parris Afton Bonds

First printing 1981

British Library C.I.P.

Bonds, Parris Afton
   Made for each other. - (Silhouette romance)
   I. Title
   813'.54(F)   PS3552.059

ISBN 0-340-27258-9

Printed and bound in Canada for Hodder and Stoughton Paperbacks, a division of Hodder and Stoughton Ltd., Mill Road, Dunton Green, Sevenoaks, Kent (Editorial Office: 47 Bedford Square, London, WC1 3DP)

*For Kit O'Brien Jones—
a true Southern gentlewoman*

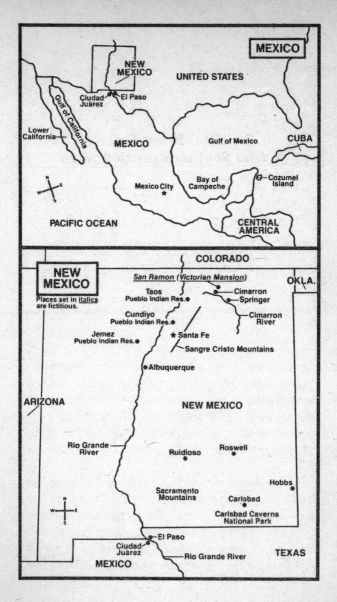

Chapter One

The last thing Julie recalled before her Volvo station wagon careened off New Mexico's Roswell–Ruidoso highway and somersaulted across the snow-blanketed field was her friend Pam McKinney's riotous laughter over one of the silly, inane remarks the two of them had been trading off during the course of their trip.

Then there came the blinding headlights from the distant oncoming car, the first car they had passed on the long, desolate stretch over the high plains in almost an hour, and the station wagon began to slip-slide across a patch of ice. Eternal seconds of frantic weightlessness followed, and finally the sharp crack of pain. Fingers of vapor reached into the recesses of Julie's stunned mind, and she slowly shook her head, trying to clear it.

Gasoline! Quickly she scrambled to her knees. The jarring pain in her shoulder warned her something was broken. The car was a cave of blackness, and for a moment Julie was not certain which direction was up or in what direction the car doors and escape lay.

"Pam?" she mumbled. "Are you all right?"

A silence permeated the darkness, along with the cloying, bitter odor of the gasoline. They had to get out! Where was Pam? Panicky now, Julie felt along the dash panel and, locating the keys, switched off the motor. From the position of the steering wheel she realized the car lay tilted on its passenger side. She began to crawl through the debris of suitcases, loose clothing, and packed food, groping in the darkness for Pam.

Silent pleas that her friend was alive blended with the urgency to escape and the stabbing pain in Julie's shoulder. "Pam!" she cried out. "Where are you?"

Somewhere toward the rear of the car a soft moan answered her, and Julie felt relief mixed with helplessness at their plight. Apparently Pam was not fully conscious. And for Julie to even move her left arm sent waves of agony through her. Yet she had to pull Pam from the gas-soaked car. Immediately!

Waves of dizziness generated by the gasoline fumes washed over Julie. Suddenly there came a bright flash of light and the icy blast of air from above as the driver's door swung open. A low, husky voice etched with concern demanded, "Are you okay? Can you move?"

Julie's dazed eyes squinted against the glare of the flashlight. Somewhere beyond the glare a pair of eyes glittered startling blue against the night's darkness. Julie nodded her head, then wished she had not as the slight movement produced another onslaught of pain. "I think so," she managed. "My left shoulder—but my friend . . . can you get to her? I think she's unconscious."

The flashlight's beam left Julie's small, pale face to sweep over the car's interior, halting on the inert figure crumpled like a rag doll against the bottom door of the back seat. The light skittered away, and the man's tall, lean figure was silhouetted in the frame of the door as he lowered himself inside the car.

As he bent near her, Julie was aware of the man's strong scent of woodsmoke and tobacco, overpowering even that of the gasoline fumes, then the frightening touch of warm fingers sliding inside the V neck of her velour sweater. For a breathless moment she lay there, helpless against whatever he might choose to do; yet there was something reassuring about the gentle way his fingers searched along the area above her breast . . . and something tantalizingly unfamiliar.

"You've a broken collarbone," he said, the long, hard line of his mouth grim.

"The gasoline . . ." she murmured. Fear of an explosion stirred in Julie again.

"Your tank's full," the man said, his flashlight indicating the gas gauge. "There's little risk of an explosion since the vapors haven't had a chance to build up."

He withdrew his hand, and Julie was surprised to find she missed its comforting warmth as she watched him maneuver around the front seat and out of her sight. The hissing of the November wind rushing down off the Sacramento Mountains was the only sound in the long silence until Pam groaned. "My head," the girl whimpered.

"Your friend seems to have nothing broken," the man told Julie. "Possibly a concussion, though."

Julie closed her eyes against the tears of relief, only to feel something warm draped over her. Her lids fluttered open to see the man kneeling above her again. His fleece-lined leather coat covered her upper torso. "Brace yourself," he said. A roughness steeled his voice as his arms enfolded her against the width of his chest.

A streak of pain engulfed Julie, so that the

transfer to the warm shelter of the four-wheel Blazer was a haze of movement. It seemed only seconds before the man was back, letting in another gust of arctic wind as he deposited Pam on the rear seat.

Julie bit her lower lip with worry as she glanced back at her friend's motionless body. Was it only moments before that they had been laughing at something silly, Pam's remark about Julie's eyes? "They're not tilted at the corners like Sophia Loren's or gorgeously wide like Audrey Hepburn's, but there is something definitely sexy about them—not your ordinary cow eyes, you understand."

Upon reflection the remark did not seem that funny to Julie, but after driving all day and half the night every word that came out of their mouths had seemed outrageously hilarious at the moment—even Pam's quip about Julie's five-foot Thumbelina frame.

The man slid into the driver's seat, and only then could Julie make out the phantom face of her rescuer. The dashboard lights illuminated high-planed cheeks and a hard cut of jaw and sharply squared chin covered with a dark, shaggy growth that was more than an unshaven stubble but not quite long enough for a beard. Beneath the aquiline nose the uncompromising curve of the generous lips stretched in a forbidding line.

The heavy-lidded eyes flicked Julie a measured look, and she realized how awful she must appear. With an unconsciously feminine gesture her good hand came up to brush through the swath of cinnamon-colored hair that tumbled over her right temple. Another section of hair had slipped out of one of the pig tails she had fashioned, to cascade about one shoulder.

"I've lost my ribbon," she murmured. Her voice seemed to come from the end of a long tunnel. She tried to still the trembling that began to shake her, wondering if she was suffering the aftereffects of shock.

"You're lucky you didn't lose your life," the man snapped. "What in the world were you doing driving on the roads? Didn't you know there were travelers' advisories out?"

If the stranger meant to shake her out of the shock, he succeeded. She had to acknowledge that her car's radio had warned them of the hazardous conditions as they left the last lights of Hobbs, New Mexico, but snowplows had already cleared the high-desert highway and the winter winds seemed to have dried the pavement by the time they passed through the small, isolated town of Roswell and began the steady climb that would turn into a tortuously twisting road once it reached the foothills of Ruidoso's Sacramento Mountains.

"What were *you* doing out on the road?" Julie shot back defensively.

The man nodded to the gearshift protruding

from the center of the car's floor. "I have four-wheel drive," he said impatiently. "And I don't drive fast in this kind of weather—as, from the looks of the accident, you were."

Julie bristled under his accusing gaze. "If you hadn't had your headlights on bright, I'd have seen that patch of ice. It's your fault!"

His mouth quirked in a sardonic smile. "At a distance of five miles you were blinded by my light beams?"

Rendered defenseless by his logic, Julie dropped the argument. But the realization that she was in a car with a strange man and virtually helpless swept over her like a Texas blue norther, causing her to shiver again. Her gaze went to the .30/.30 rifle mounted on a rack over one of the rear side windows. "Who are you?" she asked suspiciously.

The man's narrowed eyes never left the road. "Nick," he said and volunteered no further information, which made Julie that much more apprehensive.

"Where are you taking us?"

"Back to the Roswell hospital. Though it's small, it's the only hospital around for fifty miles or more."

Julie's lips clamped shut. She did not know how anything could look blacker. She had agreed to Pam's suggestion of making a weekend vacation at Carlsbad Caverns near Hobbs out of a free-lance story Julie hoped to do on the proposed nuclear-waste site outside the city. But a burst radiator hose curtailed their two-day vacation and their money so that they had to plan a straight-through return drive to Santa Fe Saturday evening instead of an all-day leisurely trip on Sunday.

Julie could just imagine her parents' I-told-you-so expression, though they might never actually utter the words. Five years ago they had gently cautioned her that twenty was too young to strike out from Little Elm, Texas, on her own as a free-lance reporter—that she'd be better off going to the nearby women's university at Denton and studying journalism.

Now she and Pam would be detained in a small hospital in the middle of nowhere with no hope of having the station wagon repaired before Monday or Tuesday at the earliest. Thank goodness she had car insurance. She could only hope that Pam, like herself, had hospitalization.

She gave that information, along with Pam's address and her own data, to the middle-aged nurse on duty. All the while she was uncomfortably aware of the stranger's hawklike scrutiny of her. For the first time, beneath the harsh bright glare of the emergency-room lights, her gaze met his intense blue eyes. There was something about them, about his rough-cast face with the dark brown hair that was long enough to curl about the open collar of his flannel shirt, that was vaguely familiar.

Pam, semiconscious, was wheeled away on a bed to another room, while Julie suffered through the agony of having her shoulder maneuvered into different positions for X rays. After the technician finished with her, she was helped out of the room and passed Pam, who was now coming in. "Are you all right?" she asked her friend.

Pam smiled wanly, her freckles pale in her round face. "This is just what I needed—an enforced rest."

Julie touched her shoulder reassuringly. "I'll call Jim and tell him that his best secretary will be on an extended vacation."

Pam's hazel eyes went to the shoulder that Julie was holding in an awkward position. "And tell him also that his favorite girl will be out of commission for a while," she said with a hint of her old mischievousness.

Julie made a face at her. Jim Miller, her boss and the editor of the *Santa Fe Sun*, had for the first time asked Julie out the week before, and she felt Pam was making more out of the casual friendship than really existed.

When Julie was helped back into the emergency room her gaze immediately flew to her rescuer. As barbarous and unsociable as he was, he still seemed to her a lifeline, her protector in the midst of the impersonal hospital treatment. *He* knew what had happened to her. *He* had seen the terrible accident. Surely it was as real for him as the pain was for her now.

The doctor on duty reiterated the stranger's assessment of the injuries as he and the nurse strapped Julie into a harnesslike apparatus that rigidified her upper torso. Julie obediently swallowed the pain pill the nurse gave her, only half listening to the bushy-haired doctor.

"It'll be a good six weeks before your clavicle heals, young lady. Your body's taken quite a bruising, and you'll be awfully sore for two or three days. I'd wear that brace for at least a month. Your friend's fine, but we usually keep someone who has suffered a concussion under observation for a day or so to watch for possible contusion, bruising of the brain."

Julie's shoulders would have sagged with the terrible news had they not been pinned back by the uncomfortable brace. No car—she couldn't drive if she wanted to at that moment. No money in her purse—for either bus fare back to Santa Fe or a motel room while she waited for Pam to be discharged from observation. It seemed even Pam was better off than she, for at least her friend's insurance would pick up her stayover in the hospital.

Angrily Julie's yellow-flecked green eyes switched back to the stranger, who now stood talking with a highway patrolman who was making a report of the accident. She heard the patrolman say something about having the car towed in, but the bad news really didn't bother her at that point. Pain, though now easing somewhat with the drug she had been given, occupied every part of her—pain, and fury at the stranger who leaned so nonchalantly against the emergency station's counter, his faded jeans molding the taut waist and narrow hips and the worn boots making him look at least seven feet tall.

It was all his fault!

As if he sensed her gaze on him, he left the patrolman and crossed to her with a lithe, catlike grace. His blue eyes were as icy as the snow outside. "According to the patrolman's report, you're the scathing tongue of the *Santa Fe Sun*'s political column—Julie Dever."

Momentarily Julie was startled by the coldness behind the statement and the expression of contempt stamped on the harsh countenance. But the doctor's next words brought her attention back in focus. "I'm discharging Miss Dever," he told the man and handed him a vial of pills for pain relief. "You can take her home now—and be sure to tighten her brace every day," he added as he turned to attend another patient entering the emergency room.

The stranger's eyebrows raked upward in surprise, but before he could say anything, Julie blurted, "None of this would have happened if it hadn't been for your bright lights! I've nowhere to go, no money, no car—you owe it to me to pay for my motel room until I can cash a check Monday!"

The straight dark brows came together in a frown. The lazy-lidded gaze swept over Julie with disdain, and it was then she realized what was so familiar about him. He was the elusive, aloof state senator, Nicholas Raffer— at thirty-two the youngest senator in New Mexico—that every newspaper and magazine in the state was eager to do a story about!

Oh, it was common knowledge that Nicholas's father owned the enormous San Ramon ranch that was part of the legendary Spanish land grant south of Taos. And someone had dug up the fact that Nicholas had worked his way through law school by roughnecking on New Mexico's oil wells. But other than that, not much was known about Nicholas, for he made it clear he wanted to keep a low profile on his born-with-a-silver-spoon-in-his-mouth history and concentrate on his political accomplishments.

Julie winced as she recalled she had crucified him twice within the month in her editorial column—the "Santa Fe Speculator"—for his favorable stand on nuclear energy. No wonder he disliked her!

She would have recognized him earlier had it not been for the dire circumstances of their meeting as well as for his shaggy beard and rough clothing. She had had a few glimpses of him at the capitol building or at one of Santa Fe's fashionable restaurants, always with a beautiful woman draped across his arm, and he was each time dressed in impeccably tailored suits that enhanced his rugged whip-cord leanness, and his sun-bronzed face had always been smoothly shaven to reveal the sharp line of jaw and sensual curve of lips.

Half the women in town were after the young senator, but odds heavily favored Santa Fe's patroness of the arts and daughter of New Mexico's chief justice, Sheila Morrison, a strikingly beautiful woman whose divorce the year before had also left her wealthy—and free to pursue Nicholas.

Now Julie looked at Nick's chiseled face and felt a tremor of fear under the angry slash of his gaze that she had provoked with her accusation that the accident had been his fault. It must have been the reaction to the drug she had taken that made her snap rashly, "Well, are you going to get me a room—or do you want your constituents to find out their representative is not a friend of the people?"

"I ought to jerk you down off that table," he told her in a low, tight voice, "and break the rest of the bones in your body!"

Suddenly Julie found herself in his arms once again as he edged his way past the nursing station and out the sliding glass doors that opened electronically at his approach.

"The nearest motel will be fine," Julie said breathlessly as the bitterly cold night air swept over her. When Nick wheeled the car out onto the main highway and bypassed several motels, she became concerned. As Roswell's lights faded behind and the road began to climb and twist through the Sacramento foothills, she became frightened.

"Where are you taking me?" she demanded.

"You said I owed you a place to stay," Nick said, not taking his gaze off the darkened highway. "And in case you didn't notice, the motels we passed had 'No Vacancy' signs. So you're staying at my cabin in Ruidoso."

"But I can't!" she gasped. "Besides, I couldn't put you out of your own cabin."

Nick slammed on the brakes, and the vehicle slid to one side on the slick pavement before it came to a halt under his skillful control. "It's either stay at my cabin," he said, and she did not miss the triumph that gleamed in his eyes, "or find yourself a room— which, with the ski season, I doubt you shall accomplish."

Julie looked away from the piercing blue eyes to the snow that had begun to swirl again outside. Already her lids felt drowsy. What could she do? She did not feel like making any decision right now. She huddled against the door. "All right," she agreed miserably.

She was determined she would stay awake,

but involuntarily her lids closed, lying like spilt ink on her high cheekbones. She was only vaguely aware of the snakelike twists and hairpin turns the vehicle took as it made its way to the sleepy village of Ruidoso nestled in the snow-laced mountains. It seemed only minutes had passed, but the trip had to have taken at least an hour before the Blazer turned off onto a side road that wound up into Brady Canyon.

By the time Nick halted the car beneath the canopy of pines and firs, Julie's mind had alerted her that the journey was over. She blinked, trying to marshal some sort of logical thought, yet there existed only the panicky feeling that she was alone with a man who was notorious for his careless, offhanded treatment of women.

This time, though, when Nick lifted her against his chest, she did not cringe, for she was beginning to feel accustomed to the position. She could make out very little about the frame cabin, but Nick's sure footsteps climbing wooden steps to a deck told her the elevated house must be built on a hillside.

One boot kicked the door open, and Julie felt him shoulder his way through the blackness to another room before she was lowered onto what had to be a bed. She heard him cross the room, and a sudden light flared from the kerosene lamp he lit. In the growing circle of soft yellow illumination she looked around her. There was only the one bed, a notched chest, and an old pine nightstand. Through a connecting doorway she could make out what appeared to be a small bathroom.

In the quietness of the cabin she realized just how alone she was with this man. "You have a nice place," she offered with a bravado she did not feel.

"Primitive by your standards," he said dryly. "But it at least has some amenities." He nodded toward the telephone on the nightstand. "A convenience dictated by my occupation."

He began to unbutton the flannel shirt, revealing the mat of brown hair on his swarthy chest, and Julie cried out, "You said you were going to stay elsewhere."

A wicked smile of amusement lit his face. "No. You did."

Julie lay on the wide mattress, helpless to move even if she had not been injured, pinned by his unrelenting gaze. He moved close, so that he stood directly over her. His eyes, which seemed to miss nothing, looked down at her petitely curved figure. "Just think," he said with a diabolical smile, "after two or three days spent with me you'll know all my political stands. You'll have the reporter's scoop of the year."

His brown fingers reached out to untie her

other pigtail, and the silken hair fell about her shoulder in a burnished cloud. "Of course, you may find out more than you want to know about some things."

Inwardly Julie shrank from the beguilingly gentle fingers, but her voice was firm. "There isn't anything about you I could possibly want to know, Senator Raffer."

Nick dropped the handful of hair, saying quietly, "Are you sure?" He finished unbuttoning his shirt, but when his fingers went to the snaps of his jeans, Julie squeezed her eyes shut. How could she ever have thought only an hour ago that nothing could be worse? Now it seemed Nicholas Raffer planned to make her the object of his much-sought-after attention.

The light seemed to fade, and Julie opened her eyes to find that Nick had extinguished the lamp. Her heart, sluggish beneath the effects of the pill, leaped with a hammering insistence of danger. Where was he? Even in those boots he seemed to move as quietly as a cat.

Suddenly he was there beside her, the mattress giving with his weight. Julie stiffened but relaxed as he began to untie one of her tennis shoes. "I don't like people sleeping in my bed with their shoes on," he explained as he removed the other tennis shoe and then rose.

Julie thought she detected a playful tone in his voice, but she was not sure. After all, how could she trust him? She thought she really ought to try to stay awake. But even with the thought her lids drooped as the drug-induced sleep claimed her.

Chapter Two

Sometime during the night Julie was awakened from a sweat-drenched dream by hands lightly cupping her shoulders. Her eyelids flew open. Nick Raffer's dark face hovered over hers.

Then it was not all just a bad dream—the accident, the broken clavicle, and her subsequent confinement with this man who detested her.

"What do you want?" she whispered in a choked voice.

"Right now . . . but that can wait." Julie felt something small and round shoved into her mouth. "Right now," he said, "I only want you to take this pill." He smiled as he held the glass to her lips. "Ravishing a sickly female is not my idea of a night of pleasure. But then maybe later . . ."

Julie could almost believe he was joking if it were not for the reputation he had as a love-them-and-leave-them womanizer—a rakehell, her grandmother would have called him. "Not enough of those kind of men anymore," the old woman was fond of saying. "Nowadays your female libbers—is that what you call them?—have castrated all the young men!"

"Grandma!" her mother would exclaim, pretending shock at the old woman's outspokenness. But her mother's shock at the situation Julie was in now would be no pretense.

Nick stood up, towering over her like the Colossus of Rhodes. "I'm leaving to go deer hunting. I'm locking the door."

Julie's mouth dropped open. Surely Nicholas Raffer, a state senator, wasn't going to keep her a prisoner! Seeing the sudden fear that leaped into her eyes, Nick laughed. "I just don't want anyone else coming in and claiming what I haven't yet had the opportunity to sample. I'll return before noon—to serve my guest her late breakfast."

The faintest trace of dawn's first purple light broke through the sailcloth curtain of the one high window to fall on Nick Raffer's roguish face, but Julie could not tell if he was serious or not. She closed her eyes as his fingers slipped down to trace the slim, graceful column of her neck. They rested just above the V neck of her sweater at the wildly beating pulse of her throat, and she knew he was taking great delight in the refined torturing of her nerves, which were strung as tightly as barbed wire.

She released an inner sigh of relief at the withdrawal of the sensual touch of his fingers, but when she would have opened her eyes to assure herself of his departure, she found that her lids would not cooperate. She would sleep for just a little while, she told herself. When she woke up in a few minutes she would be rested enough to attempt an escape. . . .

But somehow the sun was shining brightly through the window when next she awoke. Merely to tilt her head upward and glance about the room caused a jagged stab of pain in her shoulder bone. She listened for sounds of activity in the far room, but there came nothing. Perhaps it was a new day, and luck would be with her—maybe Nick Raffer, the hunter, had not returned yet.

With the most cautious of movements Julie slid out of bed into an awkward posture that left her sitting rather than standing on the hardwood floor. Weakly she forced her thigh muscles to lever her to her feet. Gasping with exhaustion from her exertion, she began to take slow, careful steps toward the living room. Her good shoulder rested against the door's frame as she renewed her strength and surveyed the outer room.

A kitchenette took up the far end of the living room, and a round dining table carved of Mexican pine stood in an alcove created by a short bar with wooden stools before it.

Beneath the living room's one long window that gave a magnificent view of the Sierra Blanca Peak there was a long sofa with a beige-and-rust Indian print. And at one end of the sofa Julie noticed a mounded blanket under which Nick had undoubtedly spent the night, or part of it at least.

Julie crossed to the caliche fireplace where a low fire burned and held out her hands to absorb the heat. But she happened to glance up over the mantel and see the large stag's head with its magnificent rack of antlers—a prey, like herself, that could not escape Nick Raffer's skillful hunting. She shivered at the comparison. For she did not doubt that, before long, Nick would try to make love to her— something he would undoubtedly enjoy doing in retribution for her disparaging columns about him. And the worst was that she did not know if she really had the will to resist him.

Julie of the Scathing Tongue isolated in a mountain cabin with Nicholas, the radical left-wing senator. What sweet irony!

Julie turned her back on the mounted trophy and crossed to the window. Outside, snow flurried over the densely concentrated firs and pines. The relaxing warmth of the fire and the peaceful panorama of spiraling trees and mulberry-blue mountains, looking like something on a Christmas card, were dangerously deceptive. She could only hope that Monday she could get her car fixed and escape the presence of the man who tantalized her so.

A freezing rush of air blasted through the room, and Julie turned to see Nick standing in the doorway. Snow glistened on the saddle-brown hair and the bright red nylon of his hunting jacket. His eyes raked over her in a lazy, insolent fashion that made her quiver inside with apprehension. "Miss me?" he asked with a mocking smile.

Julie's mouth stretched flat. She wanted to make some caustic retort, but she was hardly in the position to antagonize him. Instead she pretended indifference. She shrugged her shoulders, saying casually, "I just woke up."

Nick's eyes narrowed, as if he were reassessing her. He set aside his rifle and tossed the hunting jacket on a leather-upholstered easy chair. "I'm going to shower," he tossed over his shoulder, "then I'll feed my guest. Are you hungry enough to eat?" his muffled voice came from the bedroom. But apparently he did not even wait for a reply, for seconds later the hissing of the shower could be heard from the bathroom.

Julie found it impossible to sit idle, for her

thoughts turned constantly to the rakishly handsome man in the next room, wondering just how safe she was from him—and herself. With a sigh of disgust, she crossed to the kitchen, hoping she could occupy herself in there and take her mind off Nick. She found the coffee canister and began to measure out the coffee into a battered tin pot.

By the time Nick emerged from the bedroom, sheathed in clean western jeans and a blue plaid shirt that hung open outside his pants, the pungent aroma of percolating coffee and sizzling bacon that she had found in the refrigerator filled the room. Hampered by the brace, she moved awkwardly as she cracked the eggs over the bowl's rim. But, if she had not known how much Nick disliked her, she would have sworn she saw a look of admiration in those shuttered eyes before he turned his attention to the long sleeves he was rolling up, revealing forearms darkened by fine brown hair.

While she set the round table, Nick replenished the fire, so that the sweet scent of burning piñon warmed the room when the two of them sat down to eat Julie's breakfast. But a few minutes later, as Julie reached for her coffee cup, Nick put out his hand, palm up. A small pink pill glistened in the center.

Julie's gaze went from the pill to the brilliant blue eyes in the suntanned face. "I really feel fine," she lied, for already her shoulder was beginning to hurt from the movement she had subjected it to while cooking.

Nick sighed with exasperation. "You might feel better, but it's only the effects of the muscle relaxer I gave you early this morning. If you don't take this pill, the aches and bruises will begin to bother you again. In fact, by the third day, by tomorrow, you're going to feel as if a steamroller had flattened you."

"My agony would delight you, wouldn't it?" she charged. But she took the coffee cup and the innocuous-looking pink pill he passed her.

"You deserve it, you'll admit."

"No, I won't admit it. The accident wasn't my—" But she broke off as Nick lifted one mocking brow. Obediently she swallowed the pill, almost scalding her tongue on the coffee. "Ugh!"

Nick smiled. "I hate to deprive you of my company, but I need to butcher the deer meat hanging outside and chop some more firewood. It looks like another blizzard is rolling in."

"Your leavetaking can't be soon enough," Julie muttered to herself and began to clear away the breakfast dishes. She barely got the dishes washed and put away before the pill began to make her drowsy again. She sought out the comfortable couch and snuggled in Nick's blanket. She would only take a short nap, she told herself.

But when next she awakened the pine-paneled walls were tinted a warm pink by shafts of dying sunlight. She had slept through the afternoon! Warily her gaze reconnoitered the room, halting as it came upon Nick hunkered before the fire, sharpening his knife.

As though he sensed her intent gaze, he raised his dark head. His light blue eyes—as clear as New Mexico's skies—pinned her where she lay. They took in her tousled cinnamon-red hair and the heavy-lidded eyes that watched him with an unaware sleepy sensuality. Slowly, purposefully, he rose and crossed the room to stand over her. One hand reached out to play along her full cheekbone, and Julie trembled inside. "No, don't," she whispered.

He squatted on his haunches, his face even with hers. "I can't resist," he said quietly. For a brief second his lips hovered over hers, and she shut her eyes against the approaching kiss.

At twenty-five the small-town girl was no novice to lovemaking. Though it might have shocked her mother, she had petted in the back seat of cars once or twice, but the high-school superjock had gotten no further than fondling her blouse-covered breasts. Her virginal state was due not so much to the principles her parents had instilled in her as to her boredom with sex. If the gorgeous hunk who was the football cocaptain her senior year could not move her with his wet, tongue-gouging kisses that almost suffocated her, and if the dates she had in later years left her feeling as if she had been mauled, she felt no great desire to see what the sexual act itself was like.

So when Nick merely brushed his warm lips across hers, so lightly that she was not certain it had actually happened, a thousand hummingbird wings fluttered in her stomach in an unidentifiable response. Nick's laughter was husky. "So, the leprechaun doesn't like my kisses . . . or is there someone else?"

Julie's tangled lashes swept open. "No—I mean, yes."

Nick raked a brow in amusement but returned to the fireplace and resumed sharpening his knife. Julie shuddered at her close brush with his passions. She watched the deft way he drew the blade along the whetstone, and she shuddered again, but this time at the thought of the savagery that seemed to lie beneath his polished veneer.

"Why must you kill the helpless deer?" she demanded, now knowing exactly how the beautiful animal must feel at being stalked.

Nick's blue eyes swung on her. "I kill only for food, Julie. I never waste. There is the balance of nature. If too many deer live through the next season, they must either eat every corn crop meant for man's own survival—or starve, which is much more painful, and wasteful, than a quick death by a bullet."

Julie wanted to refute his logic, but she guiltily acknowledged to herself that the love of fishing her father had taught her would be just as damnable. She changed the subject. "And polluting our earth with nuclear waste— how do you defend that?"

Nick's unrelenting gaze drilled into her. "If you had taken any time to attend the open meetings of the Senate Energy Commission before you so ignorantly castigated the proposed nuclear-water bill in your column, you would have heard the defense."

He sheathed his knife with a sigh. "Look, Julie, you and I would find something to argue about if it was only the weather." He stood and stretched, as if preparing for bed, and Julie could not help but notice his magnificent physique.

When he crossed to her, she struggled to stand. She was still seething at his rebuke, and her caution had temporarily ebbed. "Here, you can have your couch," she said haughtily.

Nick's lips parted in a devilish smile. "The bed in there is also mine."

Julie looked up into that rugged countenance. "All right," she said, "I'll take the couch."

Nick shrugged. "Have it your way. But that blanket won't keep you nearly warm enough." His close scrutiny took in the rumpled raspberry-colored sweater and the jeans that hugged her delightfully curved derriere. "Did you want to change into anything more comfortable for bedtime?" he asked with mock concern.

Julie almost made the error of agreeing until she realized he would have to help her. Her right hand came to the V neck of her sweater as if defending herself from his consuming gaze. She dropped her head, unable to meet his eyes. "No, I—my clothes are all in my car."

"I could lend you one of my clean shirts," he suggested, moving close to her so that she could feel his breath rustling the wisps of hair about her temples. Yet his thumbs remained hooked in the belt loops of his jeans, and she realized that once again he was taunting her.

"No—what I have on will be fine." Why did she have to tremble so at his nearness? She could only reason that her helplessness created by her injury aroused as much fear as her apprehension at being confined with a man who not only disliked her but who could, no doubt, make her surrender all control over her emotions with a mere kiss. A man with Nick's animal magnetism she had not been prepared to encounter.

Nick reached for her now, and Julie almost fell back on the couch in her effort to avoid his tantalizing touch, but his hands caught her about the waist. "Regardless of how much you might detest me, Julie, you're going to have to let me disrobe you."

"No!" Julie said. She tried to twist out of his embrace, but the rigid position of the halter that bound her permitted only the barest movement above her waist.

As easily as he would lift a deer's carcass, one of Nick's hands lowered to catch her behind the knees so that she was cradled in his arms. Once in the darkened bedroom he set her down. "Stand still," he commanded, "or this will be much more painful than it's going to be as it is."

"Nick," she begged. "Please—"

Nick grimaced. "I told you I'm not interested in unwilling females."

His voice dropped to a soft, persuasive tone, as if he were gentling a horse, and Julie could easily understand how he held sway over the senate floor with his power of oration. "Your brace has to be tightened daily—it gives with your body movements. And without tight support your collarbone won't heal properly."

At her doubtful look, he said, "It's true—I broke my collarbone skiing three winters back. And I know it's a nuisance to be so helpless—to feel so helpless—when you're all right otherwise."

The thought of Nicholas Raffer having a separate life outside that cabin, outside the capitol building, intrigued Julie, and she said,

"And who tightened your brace for you—one of your overnight guests?"

Nick's brows quirked. "Do I detect jealousy?"

"No!" Julie stamped a foot, and pain shot through her at the sudden movement.

"Glad to see you angry," Nick said. "It'll get your mind off what I'm about to do to you." Reaching for Julie's waist, he grasped the hem of her sweater and with the greatest of caution he eased her right arm out. "Now bend over—there, that's it," he said, his hand warm on her rib cage as he extracted her head from the sweater's neckband.

Julie blushed at the exposure of the swell of her breasts above the lacy bra and tried unsuccessfully to hide herself with her free hand, but Nick only laughed. "Your bra shows less than any bikini top."

Nevertheless his eyes raked over her cleavage before he drew the sleeve down over her left arm. He circled around behind her, and Julie's eyes closed at the deceptively gentle touch of his hands on her back. As though he sensed her fear, he whispered at her ear, "Relax, I'm not going to ravish you."

Swiftly, deftly, his fingers worked at the buckles on the straps, adjusting the tightness in increments until he heard her indrawn gasp of pain. His hand slid up beneath the heavy curtain of her hair, massaging her neck. "Sorry—it's over, for the day at least."

For a moment Julie stood transfixed by the hypnotic touch of his fingers along the column of her neck. But when his hand moved aside her hair and his lips brushed the nape of her neck, her knees buckled with the unexpected sensualness that burned her skin like a raging fever. She stood motionless, like a doe before the hunter, waiting for the kiss that would bring the death of her innocence.

Nick caught her up and laid her on the bed, and before she could stop him his fingers had released the snap of her jeans and unzipped them. He began to jerk at the pants legs, and Julie flailed her legs in terror. But he continued with grim determination until she was stripped of the jeans and lay clad only in her panties and bra.

Expecting to be assaulted, Julie watched Nick through the sweep of her thick lashes, her heart beating in roller-coaster dips. But he straightened from her and crossed to the dresser to remove a faded blue woolen shirt. Before Julie could move he began to slip it over her arms.

"I can do that," she said as his supple fingers fastened each button.

"True," he acknowledged, continuing to fasten the buttons, "but I can do it much quicker."

Julie found her breath suspended when he knelt to reach the shirt's hem that fell just above her knees and his hands brushed her thighs. His dark head was so close she could have reached out and run her fingers through the thick, lustrous hair.

"You've got great legs, Julie Dever," he rasped, his hand trailing the soft line of her thigh. Then his lips compressed in a moody line, and he moved away. When he began to shuck his own pants, Julie turned her head, her lids squeezed shut. A few seconds later she felt the give of the mattress and the warm, scratchy woolen blanket being drawn up over her. It seemed as if hours stretched by while she held her breath, waiting for the slightest movement in her direction. Actually only several minutes passed before she heard the quiet, even tempo of Nick's breathing.

Reassured, she slipped into a deeply needed sleep, awakening only once during the night when Nick brought her another pain pill. In the darkness she could barely make out his face above hers as he tilted the water glass to her lips. She was vividly aware of his body, so powerfully virile, stretched only inches away from her. Obediently she swallowed the pill. "Thank you," she whispered.

It would be so easy to fall in love with Nicholas Raffer, she thought sleepily. Wasn't that what all captives did—transfer their affection to their captors, or some wildly insane reaction like that? But Nick was not actually her captor, he was not holding her there against her will.

Yet he was a wealthy senator, and she was only a small-town girl, a free-lance reporter who never knew where her next dollar was coming from. And he had hated her before the two of them had even met. So the idea of her becoming infatuated with the man was absolutely absurd, her mind whispered—even as her body nestled closer against the broad chest, seeking the warmth of Nick's sinewy length.

Chapter Three

The mournful shriek of the wind, the insistent pelting of the snow against the bedroom window, aroused Julie from a deep sleep. She lay there in her snug cave of blankets, orienting herself. A slow blush suffused her suntanned skin as she vaguely recalled Nick's hard, warm body that she had cuddled against sometime during the night and the muscle-corded arms that had enfolded her and held her throughout the early-morning hours.

When she found her imagination vividly conjuring up pictures of Nick's dusky hands caressing the intimate curves and valleys of her body, she mentally chastised herself. To surrender to Nick's passion would be the most foolish thing she could do, because for him it would only be a casual fling. And for her—for her, she was afraid, it would be something much more.

She was glad that Nick was already up and gone, probably hunting again. She forced herself to get out of the warm bed, cringing at the cold hardwood floor beneath her bare feet. Now that it was Monday morning, she could telephone the wrecking yard that had towed away her car and see about getting it repaired before the day was out. And then she had to check on Pam. If luck allowed, the doctor might discharge her friend in time for them to drive on to Santa Fe.

But the room's refrigeratorlike cold demanded she first stoke the fire. Julie padded into the living room, her arms wrapped about her. She poked at the dying fire, thinking how nice it would be to have a bath. What had it been, two days since she had last bathed? She probably smelled worse than the musky old deer Nick stalked. And her hair—Julie had not even bothered to look in a mirror. She no doubt looked like the Wicked Witch of the West.

It was only then she noticed the world of white outside the living-room window. A howling maelstrom lashed around the cabin. Julie turned on the radio, and the announcer was in midsentence informing his listening audience that New Mexico's worst snowstorm of the year was ravaging the Rocky Mountains.

What if Nick's Blazer had slipped off into one of the gorges that banked the canyon's road? The worry for Nick excited Julie into activity, and she began to pace the floor, forgetting her plans to telephone the wrecking yard and Pam. Absentmindedly she reheated the coffee that Nick must have made before he left at dawn, but all the time her gaze anxiously went to the window, hoping to see some sign of the blizzard abating.

She was pouring herself another cup of stale coffee when the door swooshed open and Nick came in, buffeted by the wind. Clumsily, Julie whirled about and the hot coffee splashed on her fingers. With a shriek of pain she dropped the coffeepot.

Nick's gaze rapidly took in the situation: Julie, clad only in his shirt and her bikini panties, standing in the kitchen with shards of glass lying in the coffee that puddled at her bare feet. Quickly he dumped the wood he carried on the hearth and crossed to her.

"Where have you been?" she demanded, half in tears as he swept her up and put her on the couch.

Nick eyed her flushed face with arched brows that were white. Even his beard was white so that he looked like some fierce Nordic raider. He retrieved a damp cloth from the kitchen and began to wipe away the coffee that had splattered on Julie's feet. "You wear the look of a woman glad for her lover's return," he said lightly.

"I—I was just relieved . . . I didn't want to be left here alone."

As he began to scrub the cloth along her calves, Julie became unnerved by such an intimate performance on his part. She fixed her gaze on the ice particles trapped in his hair and on the forest of his long black lashes. "You didn't go hunting?" she asked uneasily.

"No." He concentrated on his task. "The blizzard makes it too dangerous to leave. I chopped a fresh supply of wood in case we get snowed in for a couple of days."

Julie jerked her leg away. "We can't get snowed in!" she wailed.

Beneath Nick's high slash of cheekbones the indentations on either side of his chiseled lips betrayed his amusement. "Oh? Why not?"

"We—I—I've got to get back to work."

"I'm sure the *Sun* can get along without its 'Speculator' for a few days. As I've said before, you've got great legs—for a pixie."

For the first time Julie realized she was sitting before Nicholas Raffer dressed only in her scanty underwear and his shirt. The outrageous situation she was in, the pain in her shoulder, the strain of the past two days— all of these combined in a furious eruption.

"It's all your fault I'm stranded here! I hate you, Nick Raffer!"

Nick sprang to his feet and threw the cloth into the kitchen sink. "I'm going to be as glad to get rid of you as you are me!"

Julie tried to get up from the couch, swearing she'd walk back to Roswell if she had to, and Nick snapped, "Sit down—before you trip and break your other collarbone!"

She wanted to stick out her tongue or hurl an ashtray at him, but she knew she was being childish about the situation. There was nothing either of them could do about the weather. She would simply have to wait it out and hope the blizzard let up before nightfall. She gathered the blanket around her and watched with tight lips as Nick prepared bacon sandwiches. It was all she could do to mutter a polite "Thank you" when he brought her a sandwich and a glass of milk.

He slumped down into the easy chair across the room with his own plate, and Julie watched from beneath lowered lashes as he ate his sandwich in moody silence. For the first time she noted the lines of fatigue around the finely carved lips and at either side of the sensually flaring nostrils. And there were sun-squint lines at the outer corners of his eyes that she had never noticed. No wonder he was tired. For two days he had been getting up at dawn to hunt, then waiting on her the rest of the day.

When next she cast a glance at Nick, his eyes had closed and the sandwich lay half eaten on the plate in his lap. Asleep, he did not look nearly so ferocious. In fact, she would have liked to see him without the beard, close up.

She remembered him as being a devastatingly handsome man. And yet there was something about the rugged growth of beard and mustache, the careless way his dark brown hair fell at an angle across his broad brow, that made his face much more exciting than the male-model image the newspaper and magazine photographs cast him in.

As a young teenager Julie had often fantasized being kidnapped by someone. And isolated in the cabin with a man like Nick— it could have been a fantasy come true . . . if one ignored the fact, she thought grimly, that the two of them were enemies.

As quietly as she could, she got up and took the plate from Nick's lap. After she had put the half-eaten sandwich in the kitchen, she took the blanket off the couch and covered Nick. She was about to turn away when his hand shot out and grabbed hers. At the contact with him her stomach knotted as if she had been running. Why did he have that power to make her knees weak? No other man had ever had that control over her.

Nick's black-fringed eyes riveted her where

she stood, seeming to look into the far corners of her mind as if he were searching for something that she herself was not even aware was hidden there. At last he said simply, "Thank you, Julie," and closed his eyes as if prepared to sleep.

After a moment Julie pivoted and went into the bedroom, bewildered. She told herself that she should be angry with Nick, that everything that had happened *was* his fault. She lay across the bed thinking of a hundred ways she could tell him off, of how she would snub him if they ever met again.

But somehow in her dreams her scathing words of contempt became twisted with his whispered words of seduction, so that when she opened her eyes and found Nick bending over her, she thought it was still part of her dream. "Julie," he said huskily, "you were moaning. Are you all right?"

In the room's semilight she could just make out the hazy contours of the fierce countenance. Her right hand slipped up to touch the squared-off line of the bearded jaw. "Nick," she murmured sleepily. Then she saw the sudden light of desire flicker in his eyes, and she rapidly blinked her lids to clear the confusion from her sleep-fogged mind. "I thought that—I was dreaming that . . ."

"What were you dreaming, Julie?" he asked.

His face was so close to hers, his hands resting on either side of her head, that she found it difficult to concentrate on what she was saying. Her head moved slowly back and forth. "I don't remember," she lied.

One brow shot up. "Oh?" His fingers brushed aside the wisps of hair that had fallen across her forehead. "How are you feeling?"

"Fine," she whispered, disconcerted by the chiseled lips that hovered just over hers and the bold blue eyes that seemed to devour her. If he would just go away so she could compose her emotions! Her heart beat so wildly she knew he must hear it. "I—I'm thirsty, though. I'd like to get a drink."

She tried to lever herself up, but Nick caught her in his arms and lifted her from the bed, standing her on her feet. "Is that better?" he asked with a smile that told her he was well aware of her ploy.

When his gaze slid downward to the soft, full curve of her breasts displayed in the opening of his shirt, she blushed and tried to cover herself. "It's a little late for that, isn't it?" he said with a laugh and gathered her against him.

Julie turned her face away from his kiss, and his lips burned the delicate hollow of her ear. She stood paralyzed by the unbearable pleasure of his touch, unable to move as he kissed the pulse that beat at her temple. His mouth slipped down to capture hers, his hungry lips playing lightly across her softer ones. His kiss demanded nothing but tempted Julie with the delight of the pleasure to come.

She swayed against him, her lips parted, her lids fluttering closed in impatient expectation. But when his hands imprisoned her hips, his thumbs massaging her pelvic bones, she jerked away, astounded at how easily she had given herself up to his passion.

"Find someone else to add to your list of conquests," she said in a tight voice, unable to meet his darkened eyes. She whirled away and fled to the safety of the kitchen. But even then she was thwarted, for when she shakily tried to reach a glass in the cabinet she almost knocked the sugar bowl over.

"See, you need me," Nick said behind her as he set the sugar bowl back in its place.

Julie spun around, feeling cornered there in the small kitchen with him. She searched his countenance for some sign of anger, but his expression held only indifference. Warily she watched him as he took a bottle of rosé wine from the refrigerator and two wineglasses from a cabinet. He poured out the sparkling liquid and passed her a glass.

"To the blizzard's end," he said with a sardonic smile.

"I'll second that," Julie murmured, sipping the wine. Her gaze went to the window, and it did seem that the snow was not falling so heavily. Perhaps she would not have to spend one more night with Nick after all. If nothing else, she could spend the night sitting in the hospital lobby. But she knew she could not stay in the cabin with Nick.

She looked back to find his eyes on her, and once again her heart trip-hammered at his nearness. "I think I'll try to call Pam," she said, trying to edge past him.

Nick crooked a hard smile. "You're a coward, Julie. I feel sorry for whatever man it is who has your cold heart."

Julie felt like a trapped animal as she tilted her head back to look up into Nick's mocking eyes, but her words were full of bravado. "I *don't* have a cold heart!" she blustered. "It's just—just that you don't make me feel . . . that way."

"Oh?" Nick clamped his hands on the kitchen counter at either side of her. "After what happened a few moments ago I was left with a different impression."

"Well, you got the wrong impression about me," Julie said. She had a distinct suspicion that the conversation was going from bad to worse.

"Perhaps you have the wrong impression about me," he said, his gaze resting on her mouth, where her tongue nervously played across her lower lip.

"Hardly!" she countered and pushed aside one of his hands, escaping her imprisonment. She half expected him to follow her into the bedroom, and her heart was thudding like a jogger's by the time she reached the telephone. She was somewhat surprised, therefore, as she dialed information for the hospital's number, to find herself alone.

The telephone in Pam's room was busy, and Julie could only hang up and hope to reach Pam a little later. Rather than get trapped in the bedroom, she returned to the living room, taking a seat at the couch's far end. She sipped at her wine as she covertly watched Nick move easily about the room while he prepared dinner—fried venison steaks—or replenished the fire.

The knowledge that she could not stay in the cabin another night drummed in her mind, and at last she blurted out, "Can you take me into Roswell now—please? It's almost stopped snowing."

She half expected him to deny her request, but he only shrugged, saying, "If that's what you want. But we'll have to wait an hour or so until the snowplows have cleared the roads."

To wait even an hour seemed too long to Julie. She fidgeted with the blanket, drinking her wine and anxiously watching the window for further signs of snow. She grew more nervous with each passing moment, so that when Nick brought the steak to her she could not eat but only gulped the wine like a thirsty man in the desert, unaware when Nick refilled her glass.

She drained her glass a second time and looked up to find him standing over her. "I imagine you'd like a shower before you leave, wouldn't you?" he asked.

"Yes—no!" Why couldn't she think straight? "I think I would," she amended, her tongue feeling as thick as fuzz on a peach. After all, she might not get a chance to bathe until she got back to Santa Fe, which might not be until Tuesday night, if that soon.

"I'll only be a few minutes," she mumbled and pushed herself to her feet—which was a mistake because it put her only a fraction of an inch away from Nick. She tried to move around him, but his hands were suddenly at her hips, holding her as immobile as the brace did her shoulders. When his tongue teased open her lips, her knees buckled and she sagged aginst him with a low moan that was partly out of passion, partly out of despair.

Nick withdrew his lips. "You make me forget all my good intentions," he growled.

Julie clutched his arms to keep from swaying from the lightheadedness that assailed her. Nick's kisses, the way they brutally took from her one moment and gently gave the next, were like nothing she had experienced.

She was suddenly aware, as she never had been, of the sweet smell of the piñon wood burning in the fireplace, of the soft, distant music that only her ears could hear, and of Nick himself—of his rough beard that abraded her delicate skin, of the black flecks that rimmed the pure blue irises of his eyes, and of the warm, salty taste of his skin that still clung to her lips.

She wanted to know again that same exciting feeling that had tickled the pit of her stomach and lifted her to an intense plateau of exhilaration. Once more she raised on tiptoe, this time her hands sliding up behind his neck as she offered him her virginal kiss.

Nick held her away for a moment, his keen eyes searching her face; then he pulled her roughly into his arms. His mouth bruised hers, and his teeth forced her lips open as his tongue ravished hers. His hand tangled in her disheveled curls, holding her firmly against him, and after a moment she lost all will. She surrendered to the kiss that drugged her senses deeper than the pain pills ever had.

It was not until Nick slipped his hand inside his shirt she wore that she realized he had unfastened its buttons. "No, Nick," she begged as his hand slid inside her bra and cupped one breast.

But her pleas went unheeded as he swept her up into his arms and carried her into the bedroom, laying her gently on the bed. "Tell me you don't want me, Julie," he whispered before his mouth claimed her petal-soft lips.

Chapter Four

Nick's mouth took possession of her, and little by little Julie's small movements of protest abated. She hated herself for her weakness, for wanting him as she did; yet she could not deny him her lips, the shell like recesses of her tiny ear, the hollow of her pulsating throat.

The telephone's shrill ring rent through the passion that pervaded the room. Nick crushed her mouth beneath his, but the telephone was insistent, as if it were Julie's defender.

With an oath Nick released her lips, though his body still held her pinioned, and reached for the telephone. "Yes?" he barked. A moment passed, and he said, "Julie Dever?"

Someone was asking for her! Julie furiously shook her head in warning, but Nick, angered by the interruption, ignored her. "Why, yes, Julie's here, Miss Morley."

He thrust the receiver at Julie. She lay beneath him, sick at heart. There was no use trying to pretend with Dee Morley. The *Sun*'s gossip columnist could easily put two and two together and come up with a scandalous affair. At last she said, "Yes, Dee?"

"Darling," the pretentious voice cooed, "the *Sun* has been absolutely worried about you and Pam. Why, if Pam hadn't called today, we would have never known about your accident."

Julie gritted her teeth. Why had she not remembered to call in to the office? "How did you find me?" she asked quietly.

"The hospital, dear. They told me that—can you imagine?—why, yes, I suppose you can— that Senator Raffer brought you in. Well, I tell you, dear, it didn't take long for me to conclude that the senator had . . ." The voice paused then said, ". . . offered you the hospitality of his cabin. Tell me, darling, is the man as . . . much of a man as he seems to be?"

Julie choked. For the first time tears spilled out over her thick lashes. "I'm busy, Dee. Good-bye."

"I can imagine," purred the voice as Julie passed Nick the receiver.

He replaced the telephone in its cradle, and

Julie whispered, "You've had your revenge for my columns! Sweeter than even your twisted mind could imagine. Dee will make certain that every citizen who reads the *Sun* will know that I'm . . . that sort of girl."

Nick drew back. His penetrating eyes behind the lazy lids studied Julie's shamed face. "Julie, I—"

"Don't say anything! Just get your raping over with. Because when you've finished with me I'll just be beginning with you. And by the time I'm finished you'll never see your name on a ballot again!"

The blue eyes were suddenly masked, the face as hard as granite. Julie's gaze locked with his in a battle of wills. Whatever would have happened next was forestalled by the repeated ringing of the telephone again. Nick jerked the receiver to his ear. "Yes?" he demanded, his gaze never releasing Julie's.

Once more he passed the telephone to her. It was Pam this time. "Kid, you've got to get out of there quick!" her friend said in a forced whisper.

"What are you talking about, Pam? Are you all right?"

"I'm fine—but, Julie, you're not! Some seamy tabloid newspaperman just called. It seems they've gotten wind of our accident . . . and, Julie, they know you're alone with the senator in his cabin! I swear I didn't say—"

"No, I know you wouldn't," Julie said. "I'll get back to you in a little bit."

Julie hung up the receiver, unable to keep the sigh of depression from escaping. "It seems we're both about to achieve our revenge," she told Nick, averting her eyes from his piercing gaze. "It seems some tabloid has heard about the accident and the fact that I'm alone in a cabin with you." She looked at him now with despair. What would her parents say if they saw the headlines of the fiasco in one of those tabloids?

Nick's gaze searched her face, as if trying to discern whether she was telling the truth. He rolled away from her. The flare of a match briefly lit up his inscrutable expression. The tense silence of the room grated on her nerves like the dripping of a leaky faucet. She wanted to shout, to pound that impassive face, to rouse some emotion from him. Her whole world had collapsed around her, her reputation would be ruined and her career jeopardized—and Nick could lie there calmly smoking!

Moments later he ground the cigarette out in the ashtray and rose from the bed. "No doubt we'll be besieged by reporters as soon as this storm lets up," he said grimly before turning away. Julie's gaze followed him into the living room, where the darkness swallowed him up. Her mind was a whirlwind of discordant, disconnected thoughts. Miserable, she pushed herself from the bed. Obviously the wisest thing would be for her to leave before they arrived. Perhaps Nick could take her into Ruidoso and let her out somewhere, though she doubted that her absence would halt the scandalous headlines.

She paused at the doorway, gathering her courage to ask him. He stood before the hearth, one hand resting on the mantel. The fire's light silhouetted the powerful lines of his masculine body.

As if he sensed her presence, he said quietly, never turning around, "I suppose the only answer to save your virtuous reputation and my career is to marry you."

Julie blinked, not quite certain she had understood. When nothing more followed, she crossed to stand at his side. Nick looked down at her; then his gaze dropped, and she realized that she had forgotten to button the shirt, that his gaze was plundering the treasures of her exposed breasts. Quickly she pulled the shirt closed. "Would you mind repeating what you just said?"

"Do you have a better suggestion?" he asked, fully aware she had heard him correctly the first time.

"Of all the arrogant, conceited, self-centered—" Her hand lashed out, and Nick caught it in midflight before it reached its target. "You're hurting me," she gasped.

"Then listen to me—quietly. We can cross

over the border at El Paso and be married at Juárez before the night is over. A few dollars given to the *alcalde*—the justice of the peace," he translated for her—"and our marriage certificate will be dated the night of your accident."

"What makes you think I'd want to be married to—to you?" Julie's voice grew louder the angrier she got. "Marriage with you is the last thing I'd want! I'd rather be known as a call girl than married to you!"

"Mark my words—you will be known as one if you don't marry me." Julie's hand went limp, and Nick continued. "You don't have long to consider my offer."

She stood there, trying to sort out her feelings. She hated Nicholas Raffer and all he stood for; not just some of his political views, but his arrogance, his wealth, his free-swinging life style that gave no consideration to the female sex.

Yet she had to admit she was strongly attracted to him. "It'd never work," she whispered. "The way we hate each other. My idea of a marriage is like my parents'—a marriage of trusting, of love," she said slowly, trying to formulate her thoughts into words. "Our marriage would be a disaster. We'd both be miserable."

"I didn't say we had to stay married the rest of our lives."

Julie tried to make out in the light of the fire what lay behind Nick's dispassionate expression. "For six months or so, you mean?"

"Something like that—until this incident blows over."

"What do you get out of all this?" she asked suspiciously. "I can't believe you're generous enough to sacrifice yourself on the marriage altar with what Santa Fe society would call a nobody!"

Nick's hand crept out to run its fingers through Julie's feathery curls. She tensed at his touch, waiting. After a moment he said casually, "Protection. If I hope to be reelected to my senate seat next year I can't be worried about the next edition of some tabloid. And in turn you would have the protection of my good name in marriage. It would be a marriage of mutual benefits."

"Oh," Julie murmured. And with that utterance went all the fantasies of her youth . . . the beautiful wedding in white, the adoring bridegroom, the happy-ever-after fairy tale.

"All right," she said wearily. But the old spark of high spirit reignited, and her head shot up defiantly. "But there's one condition."

"Yes?"

"That I am to remain as chaste in body as my good name which you profess to be protecting."

Nick's soft laughter sent shivers along Julie's spine. "And what's to keep me from the marriage privileges to which I am entitled?"

Julie smiled sweetly. "The same thing that will keep me from tearing you into shreds in the press after our divorce—or annulment. Our word of honor."

"I didn't give you enough credit for being a scheming vixen."

"We're well matched," she retorted.

Nick tugged lightly on the handful of silken hair he still held in his grasp. "You can't deny me your soft lips . . . after all, without a husbandly kiss now and then before our public, everyone will begin to suspect that we didn't marry for love to begin with. And that's something we don't want to happen for at least several months, do we?"

Julie's full lips pouted. "As you say, then, a kiss for the sake of appearances—but that's all!"

Nick released her hair abruptly. His lips curled sardonically. "You still have to suffer my odious touch—at least until your collarbone is well enough that you can easily dress yourself."

Julie steeled herself to withstand his impersonal touch as he deftly buttoned her shirt. The brush of his fingertips against her bare skin aroused her more than any kiss from any of the other men she had dated, including her editor, Jim Miller.

As if he could read her thoughts, Nick said,

"And this other man—the man who holds your heart—what about him?"

Julie looked up to find Nick closely watching her, as though he might actually care that there was some other man in her life. "He hasn't asked me to marry him—and you have," she pointed out quietly.

"I see," he said.

No, she thought, you don't see. But she said nothing as he turned away. "I'll get ready," he said over his shoulder, "and we'll leave." He paused at the bedroom door. His gaze raked down the length of her bare legs. "Shall I help you with your jeans also?"

"No! I can manage myself, thank you," she replied stiltedly. And it was true: she could manage almost anything, but not without some awkwardness and pain.

Nick grinned. "Modesty is no way to start a marriage." But he tossed her the jeans and disappeared into the bathroom.

Twice Julie almost tripped trying to pull the snug jeans over her hips. Her shoulder was already beginning to throb again, and she knew she ought to take a pain pill, but half drugged was the last thing she wanted to be on her bridal night. When she had finished tying her tennis shoes, she looked down at her ridiculous garb—the rumpled jeans and too-large shirt—and recalled her mother's white satin wedding dress that had been stored away for her own wedding. She wanted to cry.

But that was something she would never do again—at least, she would never let Nick see her do it.

With the thought of Nick, she looked toward the bathroom. "Nick?" she called softly. Had he already regretted his offer?

He stepped out of the bathroom, toweling off his face. One brown hand rubbed his jaws with a self-derisive smile. "Every groom should be clean-shaven on his wedding night."

There was no chance that Julie could mistake Nick's identity now. The only hint of the rogue who had rescued her that she could see was the wicked glitter of his eyes that gave the latent impression of something dangerous. Without the beard, the carved jawline and faint cleft in his chin were more pronounced, along with the mocking grooves that flanked his long lips.

Gone, too, were the worn jeans and flannel shirt. There was nothing rough or disheveled about the cream-colored silk shirt that molded his wide shoulders and chest and the finely tailored slacks of pale blue that clung to the narrow hips.

Nick tossed the towel onto the bed and began rolling up the long shirt sleeves to reveal his tanned, muscled forearms. "Sorry that I've nothing dressier for you to wear," he said, nodding at her crude clothing. "But that should be easily remedied tomorrow when the stores open. After all, isn't that what every woman enjoys doing—shopping?"

"Not every woman," she snapped, thinking of her closets, filled with more jeans and tennis shorts than skirts and gowns. And with that thought came the realization that for the next six months she would have to dress the part of a senator's wife—worse, act the part. Could she sustain that sort of vapid veneer she had witnessed at some of the political cocktail parties she had attended?

The more she thought about her approaching marriage on the silent nocturnal trip to Juárez, Mexico, the more she felt she had to be out of her mind. She barely knew Nicholas Raffer—only his public image. And that she had often quarreled with.

But the private Nick Raffer, the man she had intimately shared two days and two nights with—this man had the power to disturb her as no one else had, and Julie did not like this unexpected trait of feminine weakness she had discovered in herself. If Nick had accomplished that much in two days— her near physical and moral subjugation— what could he not do in six months?

Her gaze slid across the darkened car to surreptitiously assess the man behind the wheel. He handled the large four-wheel vehicle with a consummate skill that matched his skill on the senate floor—the determined focus of mind and relaxed, catlike movements that belied the watchful eyes. No wasted motion. Even that dark face wore the same expression—betraying little, while absorbing the most minute detail.

No wonder he was a skilled hunter—and a powerful politician.

Julie shivered at the enormity of the step she was taking in marrying this man, and Nick asked, "Cold?" But something in the tone of his voice told her he was well aware of her apprehensive thoughts.

"A little," she replied, unwilling to openly admit her fear.

Nick turned up the heat, and after a moment Julie actually did feel less gloomy. Outside the car the world was a winter wonderland of white against a black-velvet sky sequined with glittering diamonds. Because of the late hour of the night and the bad weather conditions, the Blazer did not pass another car. It was as if the elements conspired to isolate the supposed lovers in their own private world.

It would have—should have—been a romantic journey . . . had Nick loved her. But Julie had never felt so alone in her life.

It was nearly one in the morning before the bright lights of El Paso illuminated their backdrop of the Franklin Mountains and another hour before Nick drove over the International Bridge to the old-world town of Juárez with its slumbering stucco homes and raucous cantinas that filled the night with the trumpets and guitars of mariachi bands.

Three quarters of New Mexico's population spoke Spanish, so Nick, also bilingual, seemed to have no trouble in locating among the winding maze of narrow streets the *alcalde*'s house. Behind the simple whitewashed walls, the home was more like a villa.

While the housekeeper roused the *alcalde* from his bed, Julie looked around the *sala*, or living room. A plaster statue of the Virgin of Guadalupe occupying a niche in one wall hinted that a religious man would be performing the wedding, something she wished were otherwise—why couldn't the man be merely a justice of the peace? She preferred to think the ceremony was more or less a farce, one of those fly-by-night chapel affairs that take place in Las Vegas, not something binding, reserved for people who really loved each other.

"Won't he be upset—your waking him at this hour?" she asked Nick in a hushed whisper, perversely hoping Nick would change his mind now.

Nick grinned down at her. If he had any of her last-minute doubts, his cynical expression did not indicate it. "Are you half hoping that the *alcalde* will refuse to marry us? If so, your hopes are dashed, for I would only find someone else. But Guido Lopez won't refuse. He's been my guest at both the San Ramon ranch and my hunting cabin several times."

The portly middle-aged man soon appeared, an expansive grin of welcome beneath his walrus mustache. *"Amigo! Cómo está?"*

Nick shook the hand that pumped his, replying in fluent Spanish, *"Muy bien, gracias,* Guido. *Quiero casarse."*

"You want to get married!" Guido echoed in English. His protuberant eyes moved to the tiny waif in the large masculine shirt. Only the delicate cast of the pixielike features gave any hint of the gender. Guido raised an incredulous brow. "You wish to marry"—he nodded disbelievingly at Julie—"this gracious lady . . ." he finished on an unsure note.

Nick laughed. *"Sí,* Guido. *Ahorrita*—immediately!" When he added, "We're too much in love to wait even one more minute!" Julie glanced up to see Nicholas looking at her with what had to be an expression of feigned adoration.

Guido hit the palm of his hand against his forehead. *"Dios mío,* such haste. Let's begin! *Pronto!"*

Frantically Julie looked at Nick, but he ignored her beseeching gaze. At Guido's instruction he took her hand, and her frozen fingers welcomed Nick's warmth. She could not bring herself to meet the derisive lips that professed love and fidelity.

The ceremony was quickly performed, the

vows exchanged, but when Guido asked for the ring, Nick, for once, looked unprepared. Then he said lightly, "I'll buy one in Cozumel."

Guido nodded agreeably, as if buying a wedding ring on a tropical island were a most reasonable thing to do. He wished Nick much happiness and bent to plant a kiss on Julie's cheeks, his great mustache tickling her skin. *"Vaya con Dios,"* he told them, ushering the newlyweds on their way.

When Nick switched on the car's engine, Julie turned to him with disbelief. "Were you serious about flying to Cozumel just to buy a wedding ring?"

"Where else would be a better place to spend a honeymoon during a winter blizzard?" he asked, keeping his sharp eyes on the darting cars and bicycles that crowded the streets despite the morning's early hours.

Julie caught her lower lip between her small white teeth. The thought of a honeymoon and what it entailed could give her cause to worry. "But I really don't want a ring," she began, talking slowly and smoothly as if to a person who was not fully in possession of his senses. "And there's really no use wasting money when the marriage will soon be ended."

Nick flicked her a dubious glance. "A woman worried about saving money? Don't," he said shortly. "I have a sufficient amount—

as your colleagues of the press have more than once intimated."

"But—but couldn't we just pick up one in Santa Fe?"

"What? A senator's wife would never do such an ordinary thing. No, we'll buy one in Cozumel—along with some beachwear and summer clothing." And before she could open her mouth to make another protest, he said in a firm manner that brooked no further interruption, "Just put it down, Julie, to one of my whims."

Chapter Five

Nick left the car at the El Paso International Airport that morning and made two telephone calls: one to the hospital, where he left a message for Pam to drive Julie's car back to Santa Fe; the other to Dee Morley. And Julie, standing next to Nick when he placed the call, could not help but wish she could see Dee's shocked face as he gave her the scoop on his marriage, coolly explaining that some months ago, after reading one of Julie's caustic columns about him, he had telephoned her for a meeting . . . and they had, of course, fallen in love.

"You should have been an actor," she told

him afterward. "You sounded so convincing even I almost believed you."

"Let's hope everyone else does," he said tersely. "Now call your parents and tell them." Julie's eyebrows shot up, and he said, "You don't want the newsmen to descend on your parents and have them find out that way, do you?"

Reluctantly Julie took the telephone he handed her and deposited the coins. The fact that she was married still seemed unreal to her. And the fact that the marriage would not have to last forever, as Nick had pointed out, made it that much more difficult for her to tell her parents. Fortunately her parents were out, but her grandmother seemed delighted by the news. "I hope you got yourself a rakehell, young lady," the old woman chortled.

After Julie had finished the call, Nick ushered her aboard the next flight out for the Yucatán peninsula, quietly ignoring Julie's protest about her appearance. "Take a look around you," he said with some exasperation. "Half the passengers aboard the plane are dressed as casually as you."

"You call this casual?" Julie demanded, holding out the hem of the plaid shirt that draped over the knees of her jeans. She had barely had time to comb her hair in the airport's ladies' room.

Nick took the plastic glass of Scotch and water the attractive stewardess brought him, not even noticing the special smile of admiration she cast from beneath her long false eyelashes. "In that case we'll buy you a complete wardrobe the minute we arrive," he said, unperturbed by her continual objections.

"But I don't want a wardrobe!"

Nick took a drink of the Scotch and gave Julie a studied glance. "Then what is it that you want?"

Julie looked out the small window at the rugged brown mixture of field and mountain that passed below the wings of the 727 like a giant relief map. "I don't know," she said miserably.

"Just as I thought," he replied and silently finished his drink while Julie distractedly leafed through the in-flight magazine.

She first sighted the island from the small cargo and passenger boat that made one trip daily from the peninsula. Cozumel's breathtaking beauty was a dream she never expected to materialize. Turquoise waves tumbled onto the whitest beaches imaginable. Chicle trees and coconut palms swayed in the offshore breezes.

Cozumel was an idyllic tropical isle in every sense, left little unchanged from the time when Spanish explorers touched there on their voyages of conquest—except for several first-class resort hotels clustered at the rocky bluffs of the Caribbean.

It was at a luxury hotel along the highest

bluff that Nick took a suite of rooms. While he ordered champagne from room service, Julie stepped through the open terrace doors onto the balcony that her bedroom shared with Nick's. The balcony overlooked beaches washed smooth by white-tipped waves, and about its wrought-iron railing twined bougainvillea.

Yet Julie saw none of the tropical beauty that surrounded her. She was tired— exhausted from the trip, she told herself, but she knew it was really from the combination of events ending with her marriage to Nick. The strain was telling on her. How could she possibly resist the force of Nick's magnetic charm, when he chose to beguile her, for six months, much less six hours . . . or six minutes?

Nick came up behind, surprising her. "Sit down," he said, indicating the lounge chair of woven cane. He took one of the other chairs at the small round table that was covered with tanned leather painted lime green and pulled it near Julie's lounge chair.

His gaze swept over her pale face, noting the slight shadows beneath her eyes. "After a glass of champagne," he said, "we'll take the customary Mexican siesta."

Julie smiled, "That's the best suggestion you've made yet."

"You ought to do that more often—smile," Nick said. "Your dimples are enchanting."

"Thank you," she answered somewhat hesitantly, unsure if he was merely plying his customary charm or if he was sincere. Then, as Nick leaned forward and picked up one of her feet, her breath drew in. "What are you doing?"

"Removing your tennis shoes—it's getting to be a habit with me." He untied the white laces. "No one wears shoes in Cozumel."

Julie shifted uneasily in the lounge chair, unused to such attention. "You've been here before?" she asked, trying to seem casual.

Nick dropped her tennis shoes beneath the table and slipped off his own expensive leather loafers. He crossed his arms behind his head. "Several times."

"Oh?" Julie could well imagine the trips he made, the glamorous girls he brought with him. Or was it just Sheila Morrison now—no, not even Sheila Morrison, Julie thought with surprise. It was herself! Her name could be added to the growing list of Senator Raffer's playgirls.

Except she was his wife.

"I come here, or go hunting in Ruidoso, when the pressure gets too high at the capital," Nick said, his eyes slits against the midday sunlight reflected off the water. "I fish, walk the beaches, remind myself that nothing can be so serious it's worth working up an ulcer over."

Julie would have liked to ask more, but

room service brought the bucket of iced champagne, wrapped in a damask napkin, and two chilled glasses. Nick tipped the man and filled the two glasses. He passed Julie one and said simply, "To us, Julie."

Julie did not know quite how to respond, so she merely took a sip in acknowledgment of his toast. The cool liquid tingled all the way down, and within seconds she felt better, more relaxed. She even felt brave enough to ask Nick, her husband, personal questions. "What will your parents think about this sudden marriage?"

Nick's laugh was sarcastic. "I doubt they'll ever find out. They're too busy with their own marriages to wonder about mine."

"Then they're not married to each other?"

Julie saw Nick's long fingers tighten around the stem of his glass, the heat from his hand already causing rivulets of sweat to channel the layer of the glass's frost. "They've each been through several partners since their marriage to one another. It's one of the reasons I've avoided the blissful state of matrimony."

"I see," Julie said for lack of anything else.

Nick's blue eyes, lighter now than the Caribbean switched on her. "And your parents— what will they say?"

"Why—" She had not really thought about it. Everything had seemed so unreal. "They'd want me to be happy. They wouldn't really care whom I married as long as we loved each . . ." Julie let her voice trail off, aware of her slip. She began again. "I mean—"

Nick rose. "That's all right," he said grimly. "If they come for a visit, I'm sure you'll manage to look suitably in love—however much you dislike me." He held out his hand. "Ready for a siesta?"

Julie wanted to tell him that she no longer disliked him, for she had to acknowledge the truth—that he *had* taken care of her, he *had* married her despite the fact that he did not love her. But pride—reluctance to join the ranks of women charmed by the rakish senator—forbade her.

Assured of the locked door that separated the bedrooms, Julie went to sleep immediately, only to awaken what seemed minutes later, though actually an hour had passed. "Julie," came Nick's voice from the other side of the connecting door.

Julie padded to the door and unlocked it, looking sleepily up at Nick. She was unaware of the enticing picture she presented— barefoot and hair tousled. Nick's eyes went to the door lock, and his mouth shifted into an uneven line that was not exactly a smile.

Once again she was struck by his rugged good looks. He had donned a fresh shirt of pale blue silk and brushed back the leather-brown locks that seemed to slip forward over his right temple.

"Ready to go shopping?" he asked.

"Where?" Julie was under the impression that only a few small pueblos populated the island—nothing like civilization's modern shopping centers.

"There's a shopping arcade below the hotel's lobby. Come on; with a ring—and clothes—you can at last consider yourself married."

Not fully, Julie thought. I am not fully your wife, Nicholas Raffer, until the marriage is consummated—and that shall never be.

But still she enjoyed herself with him. She could never imagine a man, especially an outdoorsman like Nick, going shopping with her. In the two boutiques they visited Nick helped her pick out three spaghetti-strap sundresses, a long white cotton *huipile*—the native embroidered dress—a pair of huaraches, and a two-piece lemon-yellow string bikini that picked up the yellow flecks in Julie's green eyes.

"And now for a ring," Nick said, leaning over the jewelry display case. He chose a simple ring of knotted silver hearts wrought from the mines of the Mexican city of Taxco.

When she held up her hand to admire it, he said, "After we return to Santa Fe, I'll replace it with a suitable diamond."

Julie jerked her hand down. "No! I love this one—it's unique. Besides, I'd only have to give the diamond back when—after we part."

Nick directed a measured look at her, and Julie glanced uneasily back to the ring. She felt as if she were an insect being studied under a microscope. But after all, it was Nick's money.

"May I have this one, please, Nick?" she asked softly. Perhaps he did not really want to spend the money on a ring, but it *had* been his suggestion.

Nick paid the shopkeeper, adding to the total bill the cost of a delicate white lace *rebozo*, or shawl, to wear for the cool evenings.

Julie chose an apricot-colored sundress with a matching jacket to wear out of the boutique. The admiring glances cast by the dark Latin eyes of the Mexican men they passed told her she was an attractive young lady despite the unappealing brace she wore.

Self-conscious under the appraising glances, Julie pushed back the reddish-brown hair that fell across her forehead and clouded softly about her shoulders. Since she did not usually wear a lot of makeup, only a touch of lipstick and mascara, she was relieved of the burden of asking Nick to buy cosmetics for her also, but she would have dearly loved to apply a sheen of pink to her lips for the sake of her feminine vanity.

Nick suggested an early dinner on the hotel's dining terrace. They were one of the first couples to arrive early, and they had almost the entire terrace to themselves. Over shrimp cocktail and mango, Julie sat contentedly, listening to the strident cries of the seagulls. The late-afternoon breeze rustled the potted palms and whisked away the salty tang of the Caribbean on her lips.

Even Nick, sitting across from her, seemed more relaxed as he smoked a cigarette. The brown hand that rested near the clay ashtray was just inches from her own, and she could not help remembering how that same hand had caressed her intimately a day earlier. And now with their marriage it would only touch her politely in public—holding her elbow, resting at her waist or shoulder.

A waiter brought a basket of hot *bodillos*, Mexican hard rolls, and Nick broke off a piece of one. He tossed it over the stone balustrade to the fish suspended in the Caribbean's crystal waters that lapped against the rocks below the terrace. Laughing, he and Julie leaned over to watch the fish bob for the bread. When the two of them straightened, their gazes locked. Their smiles faded in surprise at their shared moment of pleasure.

The waiter brought their dinner, and they ate, talking only now and then about small things. Nick told Julie about the Mayan city of Chichén Itzá on the Yucatán peninsula that had been constructed by a masterful race of people far ahead of its time, and she told him about the small town in which she had been raised.

She was amazed that he listened so intently to the tales of her home life, even stopping her to ask questions. Once, when she said her parents were just like parents everywhere, he commented wryly, that the fact that they were still in love after twenty-six years was a novelty. Julie was not sure if he was making fun of her sheltered home life or was truly interested.

With shoes in hand they strolled the sea's edge, letting the warm sand coat their bare feet until the next ripple of water washed them clean. A glorious sunset of oranges and reds completed Julie's first day as Mrs. Nick Raffer, and it was with dragging feet that she let Nick guide her back to the hotel.

He had promised her before the wedding that he would not force himself on her, but Julie was well aware that it was extremely difficult for her to resist his insistent attentions when he chose to turn on his seductive charm.

However, once they reached their suite, Nick went to his own bedroom with only the briefest goodnight. Julie locked the door behind him and, stripping to her panties, crawled immediately into the king-size bed, feeling very small. She thought she would go to sleep immediately, but the excitement of the day kept her wide awake at first. Then, above the distant pounding of the surf against the beaches, she could hear Nick walking about his room. Once she thought he opened his terrace doors, but she was not sure. And she tried to remember if she had locked her own doors to the terrace.

She was too sleepy by then to check. The last thing she remembered was the unaccustomed feel of the ring on her third finger; then dawn's pink shafts of light awoke her.

Stretching, Julie made her way out onto the terrace, thinking she would watch the sunrise alone. But Nick was already out there with a cup of coffee. "Throw on your clothes and have some coffee," he said, laughing when she quickly shielded her breasts and drew back within the shadow of the room.

He was pouring her a cup when she emerged, this time fully clad in her tight jeans and his shirt, the tails of which she had tied in a knot at her waist. "You continue to amaze me," he said with a wry smile. "I didn't think many women got up early if they didn't have to."

"You have a poor opinion of women," Julie said as she took the cup of thick black coffee he passed her.

The half-closed eyes scrutinized her with amusement. "Perhaps my limited experience has unjustly influenced me."

Julie wanted to tell him she would not call

his experience limited, but he continued, saying, "Now, if you tell me you like fishing, I'll begin to suspect—"

"But I do," Julie said with a laugh. "Really! My father and I fish along Hickory Creek every time I go back home."

Nick's dark brows arched in genuine surprise. He stood up and said, "I'm making reservations for a boat at nine, and we'll test your mettle at sailfishing."

Less than three hours later Julie found herself out in a three-ton boat manned by two young Mexicans and piloted by an old man whose skin was as brown as his beard and hair were white. Sitting next to Nick in an anchored chair that swiveled, Julie lazily fished through the morning as the boat rode the Caribbean's gentle waves. Though the sun warmed her skin, the sea breeze played with her hair so that it kept getting in her face.

"Here," Nick said, wheeling around in his chair to catch her head between his hands. "Hold still for a moment." Deftly he began to fashion pig-tails out of her wind-whipped hair, securing each handful of hair with a strip of fishing string.

When he had finished Julie returned to her fishing, more confused than ever about the man to whom she was married. Some moments he could be brusque and exacting, and at others he was incredibly tender and gentle, so that if she had not known better she would have thought he cared for her.

The morning passed into noon without either of them getting a bite. They broke for a lunch of tuna sandwiches and a wicker-covered flask of *sangría*. Julie found she liked the mixture of wine and fruit juices much better than the hard liquor she had occasionally tasted. Just as the boat was putting about to head back for port, Julie's line snapped outward, almost jerking her from the chair.

"You've got one!" Nick shouted. "Hang in there, Julie!"

A gigantic fish with a spotted sail three times as large as its blue body soared out of the water in a graceful arc. Julie's muscles felt as if they would be torn from her body. Without the full use of her left arm, her back was forced to strain with the effort to control the rod. At once Nick was behind her, his arms about her own. "Reel in," he coaxed her as he steadied the rod.

Julie did not know which battled more, the fish or her own emotions; for the sight of Nick's bronzed arms, the corded muscles straining with the pull of the fish, the hard warmth of his body molding hers from behind, caused her insides to flood with the want of him while her heart warned her of the danger of becoming involved with him.

But it was too late. She already was in-

volved. She was his wife for six months . . . but in name only.

When the sailfish was finally landed and iced down, Julie was exuberant. "We'll have it mounted above the fireplace," Nick told her, and Julie noted that there was a mixture of amusement and pride in the usually guarded eyes.

That evening, after a siesta and dinner on the terrace, Nick took Julie dancing. But the pleasant man of the afternoon was gone. Julie did not know what she had done to incur his moodiness. She realized she was not as beautiful as the women he was accustomed to escorting, but she had tried to look her best that last evening on Cozumel.

She did know that Nick slipped into these uncommunicative moods each time she was forced to knock on their connecting bedroom door and ask for his help in taking her brace off and putting it back on before and after her baths. She suspected he resented her displaying so tantalizingly what she had expressly denied him; what he did not know was that it was just as difficult for her to stand before him clad only in a towel, to feel his warm fingers against her flesh, and not surrender.

That evening she had spent a long hour soaking in the tiled tub. Then she arranged her freshly washed hair in a cluster of curls anchored at the nape of her neck with a red oleander picked from the potted shrubs on the terrace. Lastly, she slipped into the long white huipile with its border of green embroidery at hem and sleeves. She only wished the brace were not so visible above the scooped neckline.

But the long mirror on the bathroom door assured her that, considering the day spent in the sun and wind, she was extraordinarily pretty that evening, especially with the pink glow the afternoon sun had left on her full cheekbones.

Yet Nick wore a distant look of cool politeness and made little conversation in between the dances when they returned to their bamboo booth that coordinated with the rest of the nightclub's jungle motif. If his arms did not embrace her so firmly, pressing her small body against the length of his when they danced to romantic songs like "Noche de Ronda" and "Maria Bonita"—if his fingers did not linger at her side where her breasts swelled—she would have thought he was completely indifferent to her feminine charms.

However, when they returned to their suite after midnight, Nick clearly demonstrated otherwise when Julie would have closed the connecting door. Perhaps it was the effects of the one glass of salted margarita she had drunk, but she unwisely did not pull away when Nick's hand cupped the back of her neck, slowly tightening, as he drew her to him. Julie stood on tiptoe, swaying against his broad chest for support.

It was only supposed to be a light thank-you kiss for the marvelous days at Cozumel, but the touch of Nick's warm mouth against her own, parting her lips in a demanding insistence, caused her to forget her resolve not to become emotionally involved with him.

After a long moment he released her passion-bruised lips, but his hand, entangled in the cinnamon curls at the nape of her neck, still held her captive. He pulled her head back firmly, tilting her face to his searching gaze. "Changing your mind?"

Infuriated—not only at Nick but at her easy submission—Julie shoved away from him. Her carefully arranged curls came loose to fall in wild disorder over her shoulders. "And you—you gave your word you wouldn't—"

"It was only a husbandly kiss," he taunted.

Julie slammed the door and bolted it, trying hard to ignore the soft laughter on the other side. Sleep was difficult that night, for a pair of bold blue eyes invaded her dreams, watching her with derision lurking in their drowning depths.

The next morning Julie sat stonily opposite Nick while they ate a breakfast of papaya and pineapple on their balcony. He seemed indifferent to her mood as he casually glanced over the English edition of one of Mexico's leading newspapers, which had been shoved beneath the door. Finished with her fruit, Julie stood. "I'm going to pack," she told the back of the New York Stock Exchange listings.

Nick folded the newspaper and laid it aside. "Not yet. The boat doesn't leave for Yucatán until this afternoon. We'll spend the morning sunbathing."

Julie resented this imperious attitude even more than the passionate kiss he had extracted from her the night before. "I got too much sun yesterday. I think I'll stay in my room and read."

She turned to go, and Nick's hand shot out to grab her small-boned wrist. "You're my bride, Julie. And my bride doesn't spend her honeymoon reading in her room."

Julie wanted to protest but knew it would do little good. Nick was not the sort of man to put up with a temper tantrum. She had no doubt that he would shake her within an inch of her life if she went against his will.

Her lips a tight, thin line, she removed her wrist from his grasp. "I'll be ready in a moment," she said disdainfully as she rubbed where his fingers had bit into her skin.

It was the first time Nick would see her in the new bathing suit he had bought for her, for she had not come out of the boutique's changing room when she had tried the bikini on. Now, looking at herself in the mirror, she felt almost naked. She wished she were taller, with longer legs and breasts like melons. And why did she have to wear that unbecoming brace about her shoulders!

Nick's eyes swept over her when she met him outside their rooms, but he said nothing about the way the bikini top dipped to just above her nipples or the way the bottom barely concealed her feminine attributes.

He wore black briefs that emphasized his rock-hard thighs and taut stomach, and Julie kept her gaze on the stone steps that descended the bluff to the hotel's private beach so her gaze would not stray to Nick's virile physique.

The two of them were alone on the beach that early in the morning, although by ten the sun was already white hot. Nick stretched out on the tawny sand without looking at her and crossed his hands behind his head. Julie seated herself a few feet away and began to rub the suntan cream she had brought on her legs, though it could just as easily have been sand she rubbed for all she noticed. She was more aware of Nick's long, lean body only inches from hers. When he turned over on his stomach, cradling his head in his arms, she jumped and dropped the tube of suntan cream.

What if she had angered him enough the evening before that he had decided to forgo his promise? If he even touched her . . . the prospect made her stomach muscles tighten in apprehension.

"Rub some cream on my back, will you?" he mumbled lazily.

Julie's tongue played over her lower lip. She knew darned well Nick was aware of the volatile emotions his presence aroused in her! Gathering her courage, she knelt beside the lithe brown figure. She squeezed out the cream in a snakelike figure down the length of the broad back, stopping just where the waist tapered into the narrow hips. She found herself admiring those hips—not flat like some men's she had noticed, but firmly rounded with muscles.

"I'll fry before you rub the cream in," Nick said casually, but for the first time that morning she thought she detected the slightest hint of humor in his voice.

Julie steeled herself and began to rub the cream into the warm flesh. She tried to keep it on an impersonal level, but as her fingertips moved over the tendons and muscles that involuntarily rippled at her touch, her heart began to beat faster, and the tight knot of desire began to expand in her stomach so that it would soon snap at the unrelieved tension.

She wanted to stop then before she gave herself away, for surely he could detect by the way her hands almost caressed his body how highly aroused she was—and, unreasonably, she wanted to go on touching him. It would be one of the few times she would have an excuse to without betraying her feelings—and that was something she was determined not to do. She would not behave like all the other women who clustered around Nicholas Raffer, throwing themselves on him.

"My turn," he said.

"No, I—I've already put—"

"But not on your back," he pointed out and took the tube from her tight grasp. He pushed her face down on the towel and deftly unsnapped the bikini top. Without regard for Julie's gasp of protest, he began to rub the cream into her soft skin. Held immobile by the brace on her shoulders and by his thighs locked about her hips, Julie could only lie passively while those sure fingers stroked her in a manner that was anything but impersonal, trailing along the fine line of her back to encircle her waist and slide back up to massage the graceful curve of her shoulders.

Julie held her breath, afraid, yet excited. Her heart seemed to beat so loudly that the rumble of the surf against the beach was a distant whisper in comparison. She wanted to feel more than Nick's hands on her; she wanted to feel the entire length of his sun-warmed body pressed against hers.

But when his hands slipped around her small rib cage to encompass her freed breasts, she quivered as if an electric wire had touched her. And yet she could do no more than lie passively as his knowing fingers found her nipples and teased them into life. "Nick. . ." His name on her lips was a half moan, half plea.

"Admit you want me," he whispered at her ear.

Julie wanted his gentle massaging to go on forever. "Yes!" she rasped. "I want you"—the words slipped out unintentionally—"but I'll hate you . . . for making me like your other women."

Chapter Six

The weight of Nick's body on her buttocks was suddenly withdrawn. Julie turned her head to see him standing above her, fists planted on hips. His lips were stretched in a flat, grim line. "I'm going for a swim; then we'd better get ready to leave."

She watched him as he strode across the white sand toward the gentle roll of turquoise waves. She desperately wished he were not so virile, that he did not have such a magnetic personality or such an intelligent mind . . . anything to make her want him less.

And she knew she could never really have him. As it was, he detested her for her outspoken columns. Now that she was his wife, he could only compare her unfavorably with Santa Fe's young socialites who competed for his attentions. He could have married any one of them, and now he was trapped in a loveless marriage with her. But though he could and did have any number of women at his command, Julie swore that she would not join the throng of women who had surrendered to him.

Yet it would not be easy to live in such intimate contact with him and not want him. Her skin still burned with the heat of his touch . . . as inside she burned with unfulfillment. She watched his easy, sure strokes cut through the incoming waves, thinking that if it were not for the broken collarbone she would be out there swimming also, if for no other reason than to cool off her desire for him.

Nick's distant but unfailing courtesy on the flight back to El Paso accomplished the cooling most effectively. And by the time they had made the silent journey by car in the early-morning hours from El Paso to Santa Fe Julie felt positively frozen inside.

When the Blazer left the highway that paralleled the Rio Grande and traveled down a dirt road to halt in what seemed the middle of the high desert, Julie was ready to storm

from the car. Only the thought of a scandalous paragraph in Dee Morley's column kept
her anchored to her seat.

"Why are we stopping here?" she demanded, keeping her eyes trained on the distant
peaks of the Sangre de Cristo Mountains that
were painted pink by dawn's first light.

Nick switched off the engine. "This is
where I live."

Julie looked around. She saw only a juniper-
dotted mound. "Where?"

Nick pointed before him. "There—beneath
that mound. I built an underground home last
year—to escape the demands of city life."

Now Julie could make out on the southern
side windows framed by a portion of stucco
that blended with the earthen roof. She had
heard of underground homes, but the idea
that she would be living in one completely
captivated her. More than that, she felt a
great relief, for she had expected Nick to live
in one of those pretentious haciendalike man-
sions required by a senator's image—and with
a dozen servants trailing underfoot to make
her extremely uncomfortable.

Inside, the home was just as informal.
Reached by steps descending into a section of
the mound, a hand-carved wooden door
opened onto a large room with smoothly
whitewashed walls that sloped out toward
their bottom to form curved benches topped

with thick burnt-orange cushions. The unbroken strip of window gave a magnificent view of tawny desert floor walled by mountains capped with winter's white lace. The small kitchen was very utilitarian, with most of the appliances concealed by stucco façades.

But what most enchanted Julie was the beehive fireplace in one of the room's rounded corners. It lent a warm, homey feeling to the room.

Julie felt Nick's scrutiny and looked up to find him watching her. "Will you be comfortable here?" he asked, as if he actually cared. "I have a housekeeper who comes in for half a day during the week."

She wanted to say that she loved it, that she could live in a place like this forever, but she managed to restrain her enthusiasm and equal his own cool manner. "It'll do very well while I'm here."

Nick jammed his hands in his pockets. "Come on, I'll show you the—" The ringing of the telephone interrupted him. With a sigh he rolled his eyes toward the beamed ceiling. "I sometimes feel as if a monitoring device announces to the public when I walk in that door."

Julie watched him reach into an obscure alcove and withdraw the telephone. The direction of the conversation indicated that the call was from his secretary, so Julie, not wanting to eavesdrop, wandered into the adjoining room.

The bedroom was a continuation of the same adobe simplicity, with a portion of the walls extending two feet off the hard, mud-tiled floor to form a king-size bed covered with a large Navajo blanket. A hand-carved chest of Mexican pine was the only piece of furniture in the room.

She went to the far door expecting to find another bedroom but found instead a bath done in sea-blue tiles, with a sunken tub shaped in the form of a miniature lagoon. Above, a skylight filtered sunlight on the clusters of small trees and plants that rimmed the tub.

Julie was ready to strip there and soak her aching body, but Nick's voice reminded her she was not alone. "It didn't take your co-worker long," he said, coming to stand in the doorway. He leaned against the doorframe, blocking her movement so that she had to tilt her head to look up at him—and what she saw made her quake inside. Bright, glinting eyes, a hard mouth etched by two grooves that belied the smile.

"What do you mean?" she asked, damning her own betraying breathlessness.

Nick ran a fingertip along the short, straight line of her nose. "My secretary called to congratulate me. Our marriage has made headlines in all the state newspapers, thanks to Dee Morley."

Julie desperately wished he would not touch her. She remained silent beneath his regard, uncertain how to respond to his news. After all, she thought, this was what Nick had planned, and it was too late for him to regret the marriage now.

"And we're expected to attend a command performance next week," he continued. "The governor's wife is giving a dinner for the beginning of the Christmas novenas."

"I see," she said now, not really referring to the party celebrating the nine daily masses held before Christmas. The announcement of Nick's marriage was one thing, she deduced, but to actually display his country-bumpkin wife to the ridicule of Santa Fe's elite was quite another.

She brushed past him. "Maybe you can make excuses for me . . . tell the governor's wife I'm exhausted." She threw a haughty glance over her shoulder as she moved toward the door to the living room. "After all, isn't that how a bride's supposed to feel after her honeymoon?"

"Would you like that?" Nick threatened softly. "Would you like me to make love to you so that you're too tired to even move off my bed?"

Julie spun around. "No!" Her fearful gaze

went to the large, inviting bed. "And I won't sleep there, either!"

Nick bridged the distance between them in two strides. He grabbed Julie's forearms and drew her up against him. "Yes, you will, Julie Raffer. You *will* sleep there because I won't have my housekeeper arrive every morning to find us sleeping apart. And you *will* attend the party next week. That was the idea of this miserable marriage—to convince everyone that we married out of urgent love."

He released her abruptly. "I'm going into my office for a while this morning to catch up on things, and you can rest—alone in my bed!"

At the front door he turned back and said, "Mrs. Martinez, the housekeeper, will be in around nine. Try to portray the happy bride."

After he left, Julie threw herself across the bed, feeling anything but happy. It was almost noon when she awoke to the opening of a door. "Oh, *señora*, I did not want to disturb you." A little white-haired lady with Mexican features peeked through the door. "Tomorrow I clean the bathroom."

Julie raised on one elbow. "No, that's all right. It's time I got up." She managed a sleepy smile. "You're Mrs. Martinez?"

"*Sí, señora.*" The old woman's eyes twinkled. "And you are *señor* Nicholas's *esposa*, his new wife, no? I read about it in the papers." Her knotted brown hands clasped together. "So romantic! I told *señor* Nicholas it was time he settled down. Time for marriage and babies, I told him. He needs someone to love him and take care of him."

Julie hated to deceive the well-meaning housekeeper. "Yes, I love him," she managed to say convincingly, then added, "Very much."

Later, after Mrs. Martinez had helped remove the brace, Julie took a long bath. She could all too well imagine Nick's magnificent body stretched out in lithe relaxation in the sunken tub. Across from the tub on an inset counter were Nick's brush and comb and shaving cologne. Hanging on a hook was his short terry-cloth robe. All about her were his personal effects to constantly remind her of him her every waking hour.

And her hours of sleep were haunted by images of him—his brown hands adjusting the brace about her shoulders, tying her hair in pig tails, stroking her body with suntan cream. There were images of his handsome face—fierce with passion, gentle with concern, and hard with derision. And then there were the images of his body, which she had glimpsed but never known.

All these images rose up together to mock her now. For she feared that if she were not careful she would fall in love with Nicholas Raffer . . . against her will, against her better judgment, against all logic and reasoning. But then love never was logical, she cynically told herself as she got out of the tub and dried off.

She looked into the mirror above the bathroom counter. "You, Julie Raffer, are a fool," she said aloud, testing the sound of her new name. "You have married a man who doesn't love you."

She slipped into her brace, knowing dismally that she would have to wait for Nick to fasten it for her. Over the brace she put one of the sundresses he had bought her in Cozumel, a lavender-colored one with white lace trimming, then brushed her hair until it curled at the ends.

When Nick came home two hours later she was grating cheese for the topping of a chicken-and-noodle casserole she had prepared. He looked from the neatly set table for two to the steaming casserole pan she had just removed from the oven. Julie was so nervous she missed the swift appraisal he gave her fresh beauty.

"I—I thought you might be hungry," she said. "And there was just the canned chicken to fix. I hope you don't mind." Why had she not considered that he might not like chicken casserole, that he might have preferred eating out?

"It smells delicious," Nick said tonelessly

and tossed his briefcase on the couch. "I'll wash up."

Julie finished sprinkling the grated cheese on top of the casserole and was pouring tea into the glasses when Nick returned. He held out a chair for her at the dining table, and Julie took the seat, careful not to brush against him.

But he did not let her escape so easily. "Just a moment," he said, his hands grasping her shoulders. "Your brace needs to be fastened." And once more she had to suffer through the exquisite agony of his touch.

After they had begun eating, Nick said, "I looked up your address and had my secretary send a truck over to pack your belongings. Your clothes should be here tomorrow."

"Thank you, Nick. That was kind of you." Was that her voice sounding so polite and calm?

He shrugged. "It was Sheila's idea."

The casserole stuck in Julie's throat. "Sheila?" she asked, knowing exactly who Sheila was.

Nick's gaze met hers across the table. "A friend who stopped by to offer her congratulations." He took a drink of tea, then said, "She reminded me that since our marriage was so . . . sudden, you'd be needing your clothes."

"That was thoughtful of her," Julie said

102

sweetly. "I'm sure she didn't want me running around naked in front of you."

Nick looked up. A sardonic grin creased the corners of his mouth. "You sound jealous."

"I'm not!"

He laughed but let the subject go at that, which infuriated Julie that much more. She wanted to ask him if he was going to continue to see Sheila, but knew she had no right to question him. His marriage to her was an arrangement of convenience, she reminded herself, not love.

Nick built a fire in the fireplace while she cleaned up the dinner dishes, and she heard him a few minutes later running water in the tub. She realized it would soon be bedtime—and there was just one bed. As each minute passed, she grew more nervous, once almost breaking a glass she was washing in the slippery, sudsy dishwater. She stalled as long as she could, hoping Nick would already be asleep by the time she finished.

With the last dish put away and the kitchen gleaming brighter than in any cleaning commercial on television, she could delay no longer. The bedroom was already darkened, and Nick's long frame was silhouetted on the bed. She held her breath, hoping he was indeed asleep, since he had not slept at all the night before.

Quietly Julie undressed in the dark. Struggling out of her clothes took longer than usual, and it was not until she was clad only in her panties that she realized she did not have a gown. In Cozumel she had slept nearly nude, but she had been alone. Here in Nick's house, though . . .

She was still holding her clothes before her, caught in her dilemma, when his voice reached her out of the dark. "Julie, come to bed."

It was a command. Julie stiffened. Her hands balled into fists. "I've nothing to wear to bed." Why did her voice sound like a croak?

A short laugh and a shift of the mattress. She could make out now that he had raised on one elbow. "I stopped wearing pajamas when I was ten, Julie."

Her knees were weak with the confrontation she had been expecting for so long. She had planned to be firm and unyielding. She drew a deep breath, and this time her voice was steadier. "I've never slept with a man before—nude," she added, for she remembered she had slept with him that once in his cabin.

"I'm not any man," he said. "I'm your husband."

Julie's anger was her defense. "And I'm not any woman you can easily bed. I'm a partner in a deal we made, Nicholas Raffer!"

"Ah, yes. You haven't let me forget, have

you? Perhaps I should remind you again that I said I wouldn't force you to do anything. What happens will be of your own choosing."

When she still hesitated, he snapped, "Good grief, get a shirt of mine out of the chest if it'll make you feel any safer. But, Julie . . . that shirt won't make a darned bit of difference if I decide to change my mind about my promise."

Julie knew she was being silly, old-fashioned some would call her, about a piece of fabric. After all, Nick had seen her nearly naked, dressed only in her panties and bra. Still, she felt safer, from her own desires if nothing else.

More by touch than by sight she made her way to the chest of drawers and pulled out the first item her hand grasped, a jersey shirt. It was only after she had struggled into the shirt that she realized the clinging material revealed her outthrust nipples; she was grateful there was no light in the room.

She slid beneath the sheets, keeping to the far side of the bed. A bed had never felt so comfortable, she thought. But, as tired as she was, she could not sleep. For more than an hour she lay there, afraid to make the slightest movement and draw Nick's attention. Then, by the time she at last heard his steady, rhythmic breathing of sleep, her mind was too obsessed with the thought of the man himself.

She tossed and turned, and rolled and wriggled, until her head was reeling in its efforts to keep from thinking the same thought, to keep from seeing the same images. At last she gave in and let her fantasy take over.

She pictured herself in another time, another era. In the ancient Mexican city of Chichén Itzá. She was a maiden being courted in the jungle setting of towering palms and a pumpkin moon, with the sounds of a distant sea lapping the shore and the cawing of the nightbirds.

And her suitor was clad only in the native breechcloth, his brilliant body gleaming copper beneath the moon. He drew her down beside him in the deep, lush grass. It was Nicholas of the bold blue eyes, whispering erotic words of passion even as his lips bent to suckle at her breasts. She writhed and moaned beneath the hands that explored the secrets of her body.

And to her horror her dream became a reality. Nick's demanding hands held her body captive, chained by his kisses of passion. Her lids fluttered open to find Nick's dark face over her own. She should have fought him, struggled from the arms that embraced her. But the scalding kisses at the hollow of her neck, between the valley of her breasts, along the smooth curvature of her rib cage, made her forget everything until she was aflame with want of him.

"I want you, Julie," Nick whispered.

She sighed tremulously and slipped her hand about his neck to draw his mouth down to hers. Her lips parted beneath the insistence of his own, and the probing kiss set a wildfire of desire in her so that she pressed against Nick's long body seeking what only he could give her.

Somewhere in the passion-drugged recesses of her mind she slowly became aware that Nick had deftly stripped her of her clothing without her knowledge. She realized with terror that soon she would be another name to add to his list of conquests. Only the suddenness of her move permitted her to escape the hands that ravaged her. She jerked to a sitting position, clutching the blanket before her. "I hate you!" she screamed. "I hate you!"

When she would have fled from the bed, Nick's hand at her wrist held her imprisoned. "Love," he said mockingly, "look where you are—on my side. *You* came to me. *Your* arms slid around me."

"But you knew better!" she shrilled. "You promised!" And with that she sprang from the bed, the blanket still clutched about her. "I'm sleeping on the couch from now on," she told the darkened face, "so there will be no excuses for a next time!"

But even on the couch she could not sleep that night with the memory of Nick's soft laughter ringing in her ears and his burning touch still tingling her flesh.

Chapter Seven

"Ah, *señora,* you do not feel so well?" Mrs. Martinez asked, pausing as she polished the large rectangular glass coffee table.

"Just a little tired, I guess," Julie said.

And it was true; she was not sleeping well at nights that past week, and she was rising extra early so Mrs. Martinez would not suspect she did not sleep with Nick. Worse, the couch was uncomfortable. Julie wished Nick would ask, even command, her to get back in his bed. But her pride forbade her—and fear.

For, once Nick claimed her body as his, she was afraid he would no longer want her. She saw the desire in his eyes, the hunger for her etched on his face . . . but after he possessed her, would he discard her along with all the other women he had known? All but Sheila Morrison, that was.

And the thought of Sheila Morrison reminded her of the Christmas party the governor's wife was giving that evening. Nick had told Julie over breakfast that morning that not only would the state's politicians be attending but also Santa Fe's cultural element that so heavily populated that area—the artists and writers. Which meant, in Julie's mind, Sheila Morrison.

She sighed at the dismal prospect of meeting Sheila. Twice in the past week Julie had talked with Pam, and her friend had told her that the *Sun* planned full coverage of the gala event—photographs and the whole works. "No doubt her gorgeous face will occupy every page of the society section," Pam had said dryly.

Julie knew that Pam was dying for her to divulge all the details of her so-called romantic elopement, but her friend had only said, "I don't believe it! Can you imagine, you made the catch of the year, Julie Dever—I mean Raffer!"

Even Jim had called that week to congratulate her on her marriage, and if there had been any bitterness or jealousy in his voice, he had hidden it well. He had also requested that she continue her editorial column until he found someone to take her place. But Julie quickly informed him she had no intention of giving up her job.

Nick would probably be just chauvinistic enough, she thought grimly, to resent her working—after all, a senator's wife working might not make a good impression on the public! She hoped he did resent it; it was just one more reason to hate him. As long as she could maintain an unfavorable image of Nick, she was safe from the danger of ever falling in love with him. Heaven forbid! She felt only a deep sympathy for the poor, hapless young women who did give their hearts to that unfeeling man.

Julie finished writing the thank-you notes for the wedding gifts that had arrived that week and had Mrs. Martinez help her remove the brace before the old woman left for the day. Since Julie would have to face Sheila Morrison that evening, she wanted to look her best, and she was still in the tub when Nick arrived home. She had only time to draw her arms across her breasts as he pushed open the door.

A flicker of desire lit the blue eyes. "You make a fetching picture," he said lightly, leaning one shoulder against the door.

"Thank you," Julie replied in a stilted voice. "Now, if you don't mind, I'd like to—"

"But I do mind," Nick said. He dropped the jacket he had slung over one shoulder. His finger reached up to loosen the knot of his tie. "I mind very much your bathing without me." His fingers unbuttoned his shirt to reveal the swarthy chest and reached for the waistband of his pants.

"Well, I certainly don't intend to bathe *with you*," Julie said and began to lever herself out of the tub, only to realize she was exposing her most intimate parts for Nick's rapacious view. Quickly she sank beneath the foaming bubble bath. "Get out!" she snapped.

Nick stood there, nude now, his sun-bronzed body as beautiful as a Greek athlete's. It took all of Julie's willpower to avert her gaze. A blush of shame at her wanton thoughts suffused her golden skin.

"You know, you're very enticing with your rosy nipples peeking out of the suds like that," Nick said as he slid into the tub beside her.

Panicky, Julie tried to move away, but there was nowhere to go that some part of her was not touching Nick. She turned large, imploring eyes on him. "Please, Nick . . ."

Nick retrieved the soap. A devilish smile curved his lips. "Turn around. I'll wash your back for you."

Before she could demur, Nick caught her shoulders to turn her away from him. "Oh!" Julie winced at the slight stab of pain in her left shoulder. Though her shoulder was nearly well and she hoped to discard the cumbersome brace by the end of the coming week, a twist in the wrong direction could sometimes still hurt.

Nick's lips found her shoulder now. "I'm sorry," he whispered.

"No, you aren't! You just want an excuse to—to . . ."

"You're right," he said, his lips not halting in the trail they traced across her shoulder to the hollow of her neck. "I'm a blackguard." His teeth tugged at the lobe of her ear, and Julie shivered at the delightful sensation. "I'd stoop to anything to have the pleasure of making love to my wife," he murmured. "Did I tell you how much I like the way you piled your hair on top your lovely head?" His fingers toyed with the wisps at the nape of her neck, and Julie shivered again.

"Nick," she breathed, "you mustn't!"

"Why not?" he asked softly. His hands reached around her to cup the breasts that glistened in the water like two iridescent Portuguese men-of-war. "I only want to make you feel good."

He gently squeezed the golden globes, and Julie sighed. Her resistance was quickly fading. The heat of Nick's body against her back surely raised the temperature of the water— why wasn't it boiling the way her blood was at that moment? When knowing hands slid down along her rib cage, she remained immobile, wanting to escape while she still maintained possession of her senses.

"Because you promised. . . that's why not," she whispered in one last vain attempt to save herself.

Nick groaned. When he abruptly moved away, Julie almost slid under the water without the support of his back. "I suppose we'll be late," he said, "if I continue with this delightful pastime."

Almost regretfully Julie reached for the towel on the rack and climbed from the tub. One last glance before she left the bathroom indicated that Nick had apparently already forgotten her as he vigorously soaped his corded neck and shoulders. What for her was something very special was for Nick merely a pastime!

So when Nick came into the bedroom and Julie was slipping into the simple but elegantly designed pale blue clinging gown that sloped off the shoulders to gather at a deep V at the small of her back, her indignation had dropped the room temperature a chilly ten degrees. With frost on her eyelashes, she looked right through him when he passed her to take from the chest of drawers a white linen shirt with Irish lace down the front and at the cuffs.

Julie tried to ignore him as she pinned up her dark hair in a crown of curls held in place by a white silk rose. But it was almost impossible when he dropped a light kiss on her cheek in passing or playfully pinched her buttocks when she bent to slip on her hose.

"Where's your brace?" he asked as he shrugged into the black tuxedo's jacket.

How could she admit that her feminine vanity caused her to want to look her best in anticipation of meeting Sheila Morrison that evening? "My gown wouldn't hang right," she said finally. "I thought I'd just leave the brace off for the evening."

Nick came up behind her and clasped her shoulders. "I'll miss helping you with that contraption," he said as he lowered his dark head to kiss her small, delicate ear, then released her to finish tying his black bow tie.

Julie marveled that she felt little embarrassment as the two of them went about the intimate act of dressing—as if it were a commonplace thing they had done before each other for years. This was like the closeness her parents shared.

Yet for Nick she knew it meant nothing. So, as much as she wanted to reach out and run her fingers through the thick curls that grew over Nick's collar, she restrained herself. Once Nick knew he had mastered her, she was sure he would lose interest in her.

She was even more sure when she met Sheila Morrison two hours later.

Julie had tried to control her nervousness

when she arrived at the La Fonda Inn, to
appear calm and accustomed to the elegance
that surrounded her in the grand ballroom—
from the liveried waiters in gold and purple
who passed around trays filled with glasses of
bubbly champagne all the way to the distin-
guished governor himself who chatted amia-
bly with Nick and her.

But all too soon there were other people
eager to claim Nick's attention—the oil lobby-
ist's wife, a bleached blond who had already
had too much to drink; the railroad commis-
sioner, wanting Nick's support for an upcoming bill; and Juan Rivera, a famed
Mexican-American artist interested in ob-
taining a commission to paint a mural on
the city hall's walls.

Watching Nick as he adroitly handled these
people, Julie could well understand why he
drew crowds wherever he went. Not only was
he exceedingly handsome, especially that
evening in the debonair dinner clothes, but he
also seemed genuinely interested in the people and their problems.

Julie was about to revise her opinion of her
political stand on the issue of Nicholas Raffer
as a senator—until Sheila Morrison came into
the room.

It was a large room, filled with well over
three hundred people, but still every person
there was as cognizant of Sheila's entrance as
if a butler had stepped forward and an-

nounced, "Santa Fe's Patroness of the Arts—
Miss Sheila Morrison."

Julie stood at Nick's side and watched,
sick at heart, as the beautiful, statuesque
young woman with a tawny mane of hair
moved toward them. Her every movement
was one of sensual feline grace, magnified a
hundred times over by the sleek silver lamé
gown she wore that accented her voluptuous
curves.

Sheila took a glass from the tray the
waiter offered and came to stand at Nick's
side. "Nick, love," she said in a husky
voice, "I've been wanting to meet your little
wife."

I just bet you have, Julie thought. She felt
as if all eyes were riveted on the three of
them, every breath held in delicious sus-
pense, waiting for the clash of the two women
over the senator.

Nick's long lips curled in a smile of amusement. "Sheila Morrison, my wife, Julie."

"It's a pleasure to meet you," Julie lied, her
voice sounding cool, with just the right
amount of self-assurance . . . self-assurance
that she did not feel as she compared herself
to the incredibly lovely woman.

Sheila turned long-lashed turquoise eyes on
Nick. "All of Santa Fe is talking about the
rapidity of your courtship, Nick." She raised a
finely arched brow at Julie. "How ever did you
two meet?"

"You might say it was by accident," Nick said and put an arm about Julie's waist in the possessive manner of a loving husband.

Julie wanted to grind the stiletto heel of her shoe into his foot. His act of the adoring husband fooled her probably no more than it did Sheila.

Nor was Julie fooled when Sheila just happened to discover she shared the same table as the newlyweds. She was sure Sheila had managed to arrange the seating just as easily as she managed to hold Nick's attention with her intimate discussion of the approaching election year—though Julie would have sworn Sheila's eyes said something else.

Although the other guests seated with Julie were intelligent, interesting people—a grandfather who wrote historical romances, a scientist who worked at the Los Alamos laboratory, and a ski instructor—Julie could not keep her gaze from straying to Nick and Sheila. From the corner of her eye she watched his handsomely sardonic face as he listened intently to whatever it was that Sheila whispered at his ear. Every once in a while the flash of a photographer's camera illuminated the table, but the two of them seemed oblivious to the commotion. Once Julie saw Dee Morley busily scribbling on a notepad and inwardly cringed at what she would read in Dee's column the next day.

She was so miserable that the sumptuously prepared prime rib of roast beef stuck in her throat like a piece of charcoal and the red wine was as tasteless as water. After dinner the musicians began to play, and the governor and his wife opened the first dance, a waltz. A few minutes later others began to join the first couple, and Julie noticed Sheila rise from her seat and Nick take her arm, leading her out onto the dance floor.

Julie tried to smile, to listen to what the scientist was telling her about the world's first atomic bomb, developed in New Mexico, but her heart was not in it. She could not help but watch the striking couple on the dance floor. Two tall, beautiful people—they were made for each other. They were the elite of New Mexico's high society—rich, beautiful, influential people.

It was not until her name was repeated the second time that she realized a man behind her was requesting a dance with her. She looked around. "Jim! I didn't know you were here."

The nice-looking man of medium height took her hand. "And I wasn't sure you were here—until I saw Senator Raffer on the dance floor and realized that . . ." He halted.

"I'm so glad you came," Julie said, saving him from embarrassment.

"You should know by now that newspaper

editors are always invited to all the functions," he said wryly. "To make certain the gala events get a big splash on the society page." His gaze swept over her appreciatively, and he said, "You look lovely tonight, Julie."

"Thank you, Jim," she said quietly. Why hadn't Nick told her that? Constantly subjected as she was to Nick's roguish good looks, she had forgotten that Jim Miller was quite handsome himself, with blondish-brown hair that emphasized his velvet brown eyes; so she readily accepted his request to dance. If Nick could have fun, then why couldn't she? Julie asked herself.

Jim guided her to the already crowded dance floor and took her in his arms. Julie found it easy to follow Jim, though she felt none of the electric quality in him that ran under Nick's cool reserve.

"Are you happy?" Jim asked.

Julie turned her face into his shoulder so that he could not see the misery in her eyes. "Of course," she mumbled into the smooth lapel of his tuxedo. "Aren't all brides happy?"

Jim looked down at Julie's flushed face. "I guess it's just that I didn't know that you were seeing anyone else."

"I—it was just something unexpected." She met his concerned gaze. "I'm sorry, Jim, truly."

He smiled. "No problem. I knew you were too cute and too intelligent for some lucky man not to snatch up quickly. I'm just sorry I waited too long."

Julie's dimples deepened. "That's the best thing I've heard all night."

"Do I get to give the bride a kiss?"

"Of course," she said, expecting a brief kiss on the cheek.

But it was more than a brotherly peck Jim bestowed on Julie's inviting lips, and she was so surprised by the kiss that for a moment she forgot to dance and stood there in Jim's arms, staring up at him.

"May I claim a dance with my wife?" the voice behind them asked dryly.

Jim released her. "Surely, Senator Raffer," he said, flashing a glance at Julie. But his smile was affable as he gave her up into Nick's arms. No smile crossed Nick's cool, self-contained expression.

Already a swift weakness was sweeping through Julie at Nick's touch—the way his arm held her against his hard length, his hand holding hers in a firm possession. She knew he had seen Jim kiss her but doubted that he cared since he seemed to be so involved with Sheila.

On that she was wrong.

"And are you enjoying yourself?" Nick asked.

Julie heard the razor edge in his voice with some surprise and wished she could see his expression, but her face was firmly anchored against his chest. "Why is everyone all of a sudden so interested in my well-being?" she demanded petulantly.

"Your former dancing partner seems to be very interested in your well-being. Do you always kiss every man you dance with?" he asked with sarcasm.

"Do you always rape every woman you happen to be alone with?" she countered.

She tilted her head as far back as she could so she could see his face. The blue eyes glittered like shards of glass. Julie almost told him the truth, that the kiss had meant nothing to her. But anger rose in her at Nick's double standard—that he could condemn her yet condone his own actions.

A muscle flickered in Nick's smoothly shaven jaw. "Not yet, I haven't . . . but my patience is wearing thin."

"*Your* patience! My pa—" But the music ended, and Julie had to break off so no one would overhear her furious words.

"Come on," Nick said, the pleasant smile belying the hard eyes, their depths more black now than blue. The hand that gripped her elbow was anything but loving. "We're going home."

Julie was truly frightened. Never had she

seen Nick's lazy-lidded eyes glint as dangerously as they did now. His carved lips curled in a feral smile. More than ever Nick reminded her of the savage mountain lion stalking its prey—herself. "I don't want to go home right now." She tried to pull her arm away.

"Ah, but you were the one who told me last week you didn't want to come—the exhausted bride, wasn't it?" And he maneuvered her through the press of people, his imprisoning arm about her waist.

Unless Julie wanted to make a scene, she knew she had no other choice than to leave with Nick. On the way home she sat on the far side of the car, staring out her window into the blackness beyond. She could not bring herself to look at Nick's granite face but could only hope that he could not hear the tumultuous pounding of her heart.

Too quickly the lights of Santa Fe faded behind, and the emptiness of the desert confronted Julie. When Nick turned onto the dusty road leading home, Julie began to shake. She knew Nick would give no quarter. No leniency was to be expected from him. His dealings with the opponents who crossed him in the senate had demonstrated that very effectively.

But I'm not an opponent, Julie cried silently. I'm his wife!

With a screech Nick halted the car before

the camouflaged underground house that Julie had almost begun to consider home. But before he could come around and open her door, she opened it herself. She tried to maintain a dignified composure as she marched to the house, her attitude as cold as the tiny crystals of snowflakes whirring past. Behind her she heard Nick's easy long strides and quickened her own.

But at the door she was forced to wait for him to unlock it. When she would have slid past him, he grabbed her arm. "Not so fast, Julie. We've some talking to do."

She yanked her arm away. "I'm tired. We can talk tomorrow." She stalked to the bathroom, terrified Nick would stop her before she covered the long distance to the door. A covert glance cast over her shoulder assured her he was content to glower after her.

She spent as long as possible changing into the black silk nightgown trimmed with black lace that Pam had given her as a wedding gift. She brushed her teeth, then her hair, the full one hundred strokes this time—and still she was frightened to come out.

Surely Nick was asleep by now, she told herself, as she switched off the bathroom light and eased open the door. The house was in darkness.

On bare feet she padded softly across the cool tiles and took a pillow and a blanket from a burlap-covered alcove. No hand shot out of the darkness to stop her, no voice ordered her to halt. The bed made, she crawled beneath the blankets with a sigh of relief. She had one more night of reprieve . . . she thought.

Chapter Eight

Suddenly she was cold. Julie shot up. Her blanket was gone. She leaned over to retrieve it from the floor and saw the bare feet. With a gasp she raised her gaze, following the muscular line of calves up past the sinewy thighs and the narrow hips encased in white briefs.

In the dimness her gaze made out the black curls that matted the bronzed chest, then moved up to encounter the blue eyes that pierced through her.

"I'll give you one minute to get back in my bed where you belong," Nick said in a voice that was all the more chilling for its lack of emotion. "After that I'll force you. It's your choice."

Shaking, Julie watched him stride back into the darkness of the bedroom. Her woman's mind wanted to rebel, but every instinct told her that she would be wise to obey Nick's mandate.

Instinct won out. With her dignity gathered around her like a blanket, she walked into the bedroom, head held high. From the king-size bed came the small red-orange light of a cigarette. Julie slid in between the sheets that were cool to her feverish skin and lay there on her back, afraid to move. At the sound of the cigarette being ground out in the ashtray she stiffened.

Nick rolled over so that one leg pinned her beneath him. "Who was the man who kissed you tonight?" he asked roughly.

His face was so close that his breath, warm with the scent of tobacco and wine, stirred her hair. "Jim Miller, the editor of the *Santa Fe Sun.*"

"I thought he looked familiar." Then: "What does he mean to you?"

Julie hesitated, then decided the truth was the best course with Nick. Besides, she knew that Nick, with his connections, could have the answer at his fingertips within minutes. "I worked for him. We are only—we had only dated once."

Nick's thumb and forefinger imprisoned Julie's chin. "But you've never made love with him?"

"I—I've never felt that way about anyone."

"Not even me?" Nick whispered hoarsely. His mouth lowered to capture hers. Julie squirmed, not wanting to surrender to the kiss that consumed her as a flame the candle.

But resistance was impossible. Her arms crept up to encircle his neck and waist. Nick's hand tangled in her hair, holding fast her head so that she could not have escaped had she wanted.

At last his mouth released her lips, leaving them intoxicated with passion. The moment had been coming since the night they met. And each time the two of them had come together only to part, it had heightened their emotions and their awareness of each other. Sexually aroused, they had warily circled each other in a primitive mating dance.

Nick looked into Julie's eyes, his gaze draining her now of all volition. "Tell me you want me," he rasped, "because I'll not wait much longer."

But he did not even give Julie a chance to answer as his lips plundered the melon-ripe breasts and his hands ravaged the hollows of her neck, her waist, and finally followed the intimate contours of her thighs. An earthquake trembled inside Julie as his knowing fingers found her.

She knew she would never know what her answer to Nick's question would have been, but now it no longer mattered. She gave herself over to his ardent seduction of her body.

Whatever pain she had expected never came . . . except the exquisite pain of waiting and wanting until at last their love was consummated and her small, perfectly sculptured body lay on the rumpled sheets glowing with the expertise of Nick's lovemaking.

Nick's hand smoothed back the damp tendrils of hair from her temple. "Julie, of all the women I've had, there's never—"

Julie rolled away from his touch. *Of all the women—and now she was just one more to be added to his list of conquests!*

Enervated as she was from the quenching of her desire, she managed to lift her head proudly. Her eyes were frosty green slits. "You've broken your promise, Nick," she said quietly. "Don't expect me to keep mine."

She swung her feet over the edge of the bed, but Nick's hand was at her wrist. "Just what does that mean?" he demanded. "Your promise not to destroy my career—or your promise of fidelity when we married?"

He jerked her back down on the mattress so that she was supported on one elbow. Her long dark hair cascaded over her shoulder like spilt sherry. "Were you thinking of Jim Miller even as I made love to you?" he gritted with suppressed violence. "If so, perhaps I should make love to you again—and this time I promise you I shall drive his name from your mind so that there shall be only my name whispered on your lips."

His hand released her wrist to cup one breast, and Julie hated herself at the sudden passion that burned through her loins at his touch. "Let me go, Nick," she whispered fervently. "You have had what you wanted."

Still his hand caressed her, lazily circling one turgid nipple with his index finger. "And not what you wanted, also?" he asked softly. "Will you not listen to me? Won't you give me a—"

"No!" she spat. "You forget, I know too well how eloquent the senator is with words. But *I* won't be swayed like your other sheep. One day, Nicholas Raffer, I'll prove my own eloquence with the written word!"

She fled from him then, seeking the asylum of the couch. She half expected him to chase her down, as the lion does the gazelle, and reclaim her. But he did not, and at last, dry-eyed, she fell into a deep sleep of exhaustion.

When she awakened, it was nearly eleven. Nick was gone. She remembered him mentioning the day before having a client to see. No doubt the client was Sheila, Julie thought grimly.

But that supposition was proven wrong an hour later as Julie folded and put away the blankets, glad that it was Mrs. Martinez's day off. The doorbell rang, and Julie, wearing jeans and a gray sweatshirt, answered it, to find Sheila standing there, elegantly wrapped in a red fox fur. The woman's finely plucked brows arched in amusement as her critical gaze swept over Julie's bare feet and disheveled hair tied, as usual, in pig tails.

"I was hoping I'd catch you two at home," Sheila said. She turned her head to let her glance sweep the terrain behind her, adding, "But I don't see Nick's car."

"He's with a client," Julie said, still holding the doorknob. The last person she wanted to see that day was Sheila Morrison.

"Well, in that case"—Sheila held out a silver-and-white-wrapped box—"I wanted to give you two a wedding gift."

"Oh," Julie said. She felt extremely ill mannered before Sheila's gracious gesture. And though there was something about the woman she did not like (admit it, she scolded herself—you're jealous that of all the women Nick's had, only Sheila Morrison has been able to hold his interest), she felt compelled to invite the woman inside in view of her generosity and thoughtfulness.

Sheila dropped her fur negligently across the couch in a careless gesture of one who is accustomed to expensive items. "Could I get you a cup of coffee?" Julie offered, hoping the woman would not stay long.

"That's all right," Sheila said sweetly. "I can help myself. I know where everything is.

Besides, you must be tired." She looked at Julie now with a knowing smile playing about her lips, reminding Julie of the Cheshire cat. "I know how that is, too. Nick can certainly drain your energies after a night of love, can't he?"

Julie bristled. "Is that what you call it? I think Nick called the affairs before our marriage 'sleeping around.'" With a saccharine smile that more resembled a grin of triumph Julie laid the gift on the coffee table. What she wanted to do was toss it in the fireplace.

Sheila picked up her fur coat. "I can see that this is not going to be one of those pleasant conversations you have over a cup of coffee," she said icily.

"On that we agree."

Sheila paused at the door, her manicured hand resting on the knob. "I ought to warn you that if you really love Nick, Mrs. Raffer, you won't stand in his way. He quite possibly could be the next governor of New Mexico. Oh, the critics and his opponents claim he's too young, with only one term in the senate. But with my influence, and my father's backing, Nick has a very good chance of winning the governor's race."

"And you're implying that with me as his wife—"

"You'd only hamper him—an unsophisticated little working girl. It's been obvious to everyone for months that Nick and I were made for each other. If you love him, Mrs. Raffer, you'll let him go."

Julie stood there long after Sheila had closed the door. She wanted to scream after her, "But I *don't* love him!" But pride held her tongue.

The ring of the telephone broke her trance. It was Pam. "Oh, Pam," she cried, "it's so good to hear your voice!" In the midst of Nick's whirlwind courtship and marriage Julie had forgotten how much she enjoyed Pam's easygoing banter. "I promise I'll tell you everything this time," she hedged. "Yes, lunch will be fine. Give me forty-five minutes."

Within twenty minutes Julie had changed into a kelly green wool circular skirt and matching sweater with brown leather boots. She brushed out her hair until it fell over her shoulders in feathery wisps and added some mascara and frosted apricot lipstick. A searching glance in the mirror told her that, though she would never be as sleekly sophisticated as Sheila Morrison, she did look quite attractive.

Julie peered closer at her reflection, wondering if one could tell by the shadowy eyes or the passion-swollen lips that she was any different that morning than the day before. Was there a mark somewhere on her for everyone to see, like Cain's, that Nick had made her his?

Exactly forty-five minutes later Julie arrived in the parking lot of The Bull Ring, a Mexican restaurant within walking distance of the state's circular capitol.

Inside, the restaurant was crowded, mostly with politicians. Loud shouts of greeting were traded back and forth when recognized lobbyists and legislators came in, accompanied by handshaking and backslapping. It was a lively place, especially during the noon hour.

Julie recognized Pam at a corner table, but it was not until she had made her way there that she realized someone was with Pam.

"Hi, Julie!" Pam called. "My boss has offered to buy my lunch," she said, indicating Jim sitting across from her, "and I couldn't pass it up."

Julie took a seat between Jim and her friend. "Hello, Jim," she said lightly. "Are you out gathering secret political info for a big scoop?"

"This would be the place to get the latest news," he said with a genuine smile, "but Pam conned me into buying the lunches." He winked at Julie and added, "She claims it's National Secretary Week."

Pam grimaced at her boss, but before she could make a retort, a waiter came to take their order. For once, Julie, shaken by the events of the night before and then Sheila's visit that morning, ordered a drink, a margarita, along with Pam and Jim.

For a while the three made only small talk about the office gossip, the new ski facilities at Angel Fire, the discovery of helium on one of the nearby Indian reservations.

"So how's marriage going?" Pam asked as they finished the last of the nachos and another round of margaritas.

Julie bit into the crunchy tortilla topped with melted cheese and chopped jalapeños. Her eyes watered, but not from the spicy-hot chili pepper. Why not tell them? she asked herself. These two were her friends. "I'm afraid it's over before it's begun," she said, swallowing the lump in her throat.

Pam's hazel eyes widened, making her usually bright freckles pale in comparison. "Oh, Julie, everyone has those little lovers' tiffs," she said, trying to console her friend.

Julie closed her eyes against the room that had started to shift. She really should not have drunk a second margarita. When she opened them, Jim was looking at her with concern. He laid his hand over hers. "Is there anything I can do, Julie?"

She looked up at his kind face, but her gaze went past him to see the tall, dark man standing in the arched doorway. Nick's harsh gaze raked over Julie and Jim with contempt before he turned on his heel and left.

Julie wanted to jump up and run after him.

For in that split second she knew she was in love with Nicholas Raffer. She did not know when she had first begun to be or how or why. She just knew that her heart belonged irrevocably to Nick.

And now she could only guess what he must think of her, sitting at the table with Jim holding her hand. Even if he had noticed Pam with them, the least his nimble brain could conclude was that she was preparing to write the scathing articles about him that she had threatened to do.

"Julie, is there anything I can do?" Jim repeated now, with serious worry at the tortured expression she wore.

Julie shook her head as though trying to shake Nick from her mind . . . and knew that was something she would never really be able to do. He had left the imprint of his personality and his possession of her on her mind as surely as if he had burned his name into her heart with a branding iron.

"No, Jim, I appreciate your offer, but there's nothing you can do. I'm sure—" She took a deep breath to hold back the tears that were welling inside. "I'm sure that everything will work out for the best."

"How about coming by after lunch and seeing the rest of the gang at the office?" Pam suggested with a lightness in her voice that none of the three really felt.

"No—I guess I better get on back home,"

Julie temporized. "There's a lot I have to catch up on."

But she did not drive straight home. She drove aimlessly out along the winding Cerro Gordo road. Before she realized it, she found she was on the narrow Highway 64 that was jammed with other cars bound for the Pueblo Indian reservations that rimmed Santa Fe, for at that time of year many families spent their winter vacations in Santa Fe, skiing and sightseeing.

Julie pulled over into the paved area designated for parking, but she remained sitting in her car, watching the tourists as they flocked to photograph the Tesuque kiva, the round ceremonial structure of sandstone that was partly underground, or purchase pottery and paintings displayed on colorful blankets about the plaza. Not too far away a father posed his wife and three children with an old Indian woman dressed in the native costume of velveteen blouse over a calico skirt while he snapped pictures, and Julie felt the deep yearning gnawing in her to be part of a family like that—to have a husband to laugh with and children to love.

Was there any chance for her and Nick to have such a family?

Julie sat behind the wheel, trying to think clearly, logically. The war that raged between her heart and her brain did not make it easy

for her. Her brain reminded her that Nick
would never love any woman. Had he not told
her as much . . . that the dissolution of his
parents' marriage had hardened him against
marriage? Her heart whispered that with
time she might be able to make him love her.

She did know that if she were to ask her
parents what to do, they would tell her to
listen to her heart. And with that last thought,
she switched on the car's engine and headed
back to Santa Fe and Nick.

As long as there was hope, she would wait
for his love.

Chapter Nine

Over the following days Julie often wondered if her hope that Nick might someday come to love her was nothing but a fool's dream. They slept together in Nick's king-size bed, but never did they touch. Julie would have been more miserable than she was, but she kept busy, either working on her column or shopping and wrapping Christmas gifts to mail to her friends and family back home. She agonized over what to get Nick and finally settled on a little-known brand of fishing reel that her father swore by.

While Nick had not exploded at her in anger the afternoon she returned from the luncheon with Pam and Jim, neither did he exhibit the warm, affectionate manner he had occasionally displayed in Cozumel.

Only once was the subject of Jim Miller even touched on. It occurred one morning two days before Christmas when Julie's "Speculator" column appeared in the *Sun* for the first time since her marriage. Anxiously she waited as Nick scanned the column. Would he forbid her, in that cool, autocratic way he had, to write any more articles, or would he go further and openly accuse her of having an affair with her editor? She almost wished he would show some sign of jealousy. Any emotion was better than his indifference.

He did neither. When he finished the column, he took a drink of coffee. His eyes studied her over the rim of his cup, and under his close scrutiny Julie could only toy with the scrambled eggs she had prepared in the Mexican style of *huevos rancheros*.

"It's good," Nick said finally. "Your column. I've been against Senator Follet's strip-mining bill from the start, but I could never have worded my protest as succinctly as you did in your column."

Julie's eyes widened at Nick's words of praise. When she had written the column, she had had no idea how Nick stood on the bill. If anything, she would have supposed he was for it. But, regardless, she had written how she honestly felt about the bill. "Then you don't mind if I continue with my column?"

"Not in the least. I'm pleased to see you don't plan to let your clever mind atrophy simply because you have married."

He laid aside the newspaper and said, "Julie, several of the legislators have approached me about throwing my hat in the ring for the governor's race next year. How do you feel about it?"

Julie looked at Nick in surprise that he would consult her about his plans for the future. Was she to figure in his future, or was it merely wishful thinking on her part? She swallowed a gulp of orange juice before answering. "If that's what you want, then I think you should go ahead and announce your candidacy."

"Sheila felt the same way," Nick said, still watching Julie closely. "She's volunteered her services for my campaign committee if I decide to run."

Julie looked away, unable to meet Nick's observant gaze. "That's nice," she said dryly. "You two obviously work well together." She laid her napkin beside her plate and rose. "Excuse me. I—I have to get back to work on my next column."

Nick stood up also. "I'll be home early this afternoon. I thought we'd run up to San Ramon for the weekend and celebrate Christmas Eve with my grandmother. I'd like you to meet her. I think you two would like each other."

The fact that Nick wanted her to spend Christmas with him in a familylike setting offered some hope to Julie, though it did not lessen the hurt of hearing Sheila's name on his lips that morning. Nevertheless, she was not going to give up hope, and after she had prepared the first draft of the following week's column, she spent the rest of the afternoon getting ready for the weekend trip.

She wanted to look especially nice, and she chose a soft pink woolen sweater with matching slacks to wear on the trip up to the San Ramon ranch. Apparently she succeeded in her effort, for not too long after they left Santa Fe behind them and began the climb up through the Sangre de Cristo Mountains toward Taos Nick said, "You look lovely, Julie. Not only will my grandmother approve of you, but she'll want to know why I didn't marry you before I did."

"I wouldn't think two days is too long a courtship," Julie said wryly.

Nick chuckled. "It must hold the state record at least."

The playful banter between them seemed to set the mood for the rest of the journey, and for the first time since Cozumel Julie relaxed in Nick's presence and enjoyed the breathtaking scenery. She had never been to Taos and found the mountain hamlet held the same old-world charm as the central, older section of Sante Fe. Almost all the homes and commercial buildings were of adobe, giving the town an atmosphere of being encapsulated there by the mountains against civilization's progress. She could well understand why people like Kit Carson and D. H. Lawrence had sought out Taos as a hideaway.

Outside Taos they passed the four- and five-story-high abode structures where Pueblo Indians had lived since prehistoric times; then the road began to climb again to dizzying heights before it dropped down through the sheer walls of Cimarron Canyon and into the lush valley of the San Ramon land grant.

The sun was hanging low over the serrated mountains by the time Nick turned off onto a meandering gravel drive that paralleled a narrow mountain creek. At the top of a hill the San Ramon house came into view. The dying sunlight fell on the old Victorian mansion, tingeing the house's turrets and dormer windows with a warm purple glow. "Oh, Nick, it's beautiful," Julie breathed. "I don't see why you don't come here more often."

"I wouldn't come here at all if it weren't for my grandmother," Nick said grimly as he parked the car in the carriage house that had been converted to a garage.

Julie ached to reach out and smooth away the harsh lines at either side of Nick's lips, but she knew she could not betray her feelings for him or she would become just another one of the women he had grown tired of and eventually discarded.

The old woman with the silver-gray hair who stood regally on the veranda bore a great resemblance to Nick. Her face possessed the same strong lines as his, and Julie discovered that the blue-gray eyes sparkled with the same fascinating warmth as Nick's.

Nick hugged the old woman with obvious affection. "Grandmother, I want you to meet my wife, Julie."

Elizabeth Waggoner flashed Julie a mischievous smile. "So this is the lovely lady I read about in the newspaper. What was it that Dee Morley wrote—'the siren whose song has lured Nicholas Raffer into the perilous sea of matrimony'?"

Julie blushed. "I've never thought of myself as a siren, Mrs. Waggoner."

"Please call me Grandmother," the old woman said, leading Julie inside. "Maybe you're not quite the siren, then, but certainly an enchantress to have captured Nick. I was afraid my grandson was never going to fall in love."

Julie's gaze flicked to Nick, who was shrugging out of his cowhide jacket. But Nick made no effort to refute his grandmother's statement. Instead he laughed. "The truth is, Grandmother never approved of any of the women I dated, Julie."

"Frivolous, empty-headed creatures they all were. But I've been reading Julie's column for several years now. Your wife has a head on her beautiful shoulders, Nicholas. And she's not afraid to call the balls like she sees them, is she?"

Nick flashed Julie a roguish smile as he tucked his plaid shirt into his Levi's. "I think you could safely say that, Grandmother."

Elizabeth took Julie through the elegantly furnished rooms that whispered of a bygone era and showed the couple to their bedroom, which had been restored as it actually was when Elizabeth's parents had the room.

"I always dreamed of having a room like this," Julie said as her gaze traveled over the calico-papered walls, the hand-carved four-poster bed and the maple washstand. Her eyes strayed back to the four-poster, smaller than Nick's king-size bed, that she and Nick would be sharing. How much longer could she stand being so near to him, touching him, wanting him . . . but not having him? And an insidious voice inside her asked if it was Sheila Morrison who was the recipient of his caresses for the present.

Julie had thought she would feel out of place at the legendary San Ramon mansion, but after the first few moments Elizabeth put her at ease with her interesting tales of what the place had been like when kerosene lamps were still used and water was pumped at the kitchen sink—"which wasn't so long ago, mind you," Elizabeth said.

With the help of Marta, a large Mexican woman who had been with the family for years, Elizabeth had prepared a dish indigenous to New Mexico when it was still a territory—mutton stew and baked squash topped with red chilies, and for desert an apricot cobbler. Over dinner the conversation between Elizabeth, Nick, and Julie revolved around such stimulating subjects as the state's fiscal and monetary responsibility and the importance of supporting the Indian arts, so that by the time dinner was over and Nick had finished his cigarette, Julie felt as if she belonged, as if she were truly a part of the family.

Yet, when it came time for bed, Nick lingered, discussing with his grandmother improvements that needed to be made on the ranch. And Julie found herself lying in the four-poster alone. She meant to stay awake to wait for Nick in hopes they might reconcile their ill-started marriage. Just one word of love from Nick, some sign that he cared, was all she wanted. But the mattress, an old-fashioned kind stuffed with fluffy wool, lulled Julie to sleep within minutes, and she was unaware of what time Nick finally came to bed.

The next morning was Christmas Eve day, and Julie learned that Nick had arisen and left before she awoke to talk with some of the ranchhands. She helped Elizabeth and Marta in the kitchen as they prepared the traditional turkey dinner. Marta, her round brown face beaming, told tales of Nick's boyhood pranks that kept Julie laughing.

Dinner was just as enjoyable, and afterward Julie surprised Elizabeth with a bottle of White Shoulders cologne. She had intended it as a Christmas gift for Pam, but since Nick had not given her much warning about the trip, it was the only gift she could come up with on the spur of the moment.

Elizabeth looked touched by Julie's thoughtfulness. "You know, Nick never warns me when he's going to come, so I can't tell you how happy he made me, Julie, when he phoned yesterday to tell me he was bringing you." She leaned over and pecked Julie on the cheek. "You're the kind of granddaughter I always hoped to have in the family."

Affected by the woman's sincerity, Julie looked away to find Nick warmly regarding her. "Come on," he said, taking her hand, "let's get the kinks out of our muscles. We'll saddle up two of the horses and ride some of the land."

Julie changed into an old pair of jeans and a white turtleneck sweater she had brought along with a new pair of western boots and a suede jacket with fleece lining. Just before she left the bedroom she brushed her hair so that it feathered back from her face and added a hint of raspberry lipstick.

Nick was waiting for her on the veranda, his hands jammed into his worn cowhide jacket against the cold. The dusty gray Stetson he wore was pulled low over his eyes. "Ready?" he asked, his gaze raking over her in an appreciative manner.

Julie nodded, warming under his obvious male scrutiny. She turned to descend the steps, and Nick said, "Just a minute."

She turned back, her eyes questioning. Nick removed his Stetson and, gathering Julie's shoulder-length hair in hand, set the Stetson on her head. He tucked the remaining stray wisps up inside the hatband, saying, "It'll keep you much warmer."

"What about you?" Julie asked, thrilling at his nearness, at the feel of his warm breath tingling her face and his hands lingering at her neck.

Nick pulled his collar up around his ears with a smile. "You forget, I'm used to these winters. Rarely a weekend goes by during the winter that I'm not out hunting in Ruidoso or riding the range here at San Ramon."

The two horses they rode, a roan and a paint, pranced over the night's light layer of snow, their breath steaming about their nostrils. For a quarter of an hour or so Julie and Nick rode in silence as they followed a barely visible cow trail that led to a stock tank frozen over about the edges. The utter quietness of the winter morning, the majestic beauty of the deep purple mountains and towering pines that isolated the area, stirred Julie's soul, as Nick's nearness stirred her heart.

Occasionally their legs would brush as their mounts were forced to pass close when the trail suddenly narrowed, and Julie's breath would catch, the sudden cold air searing her throat. Once, when Nick dropped back on the trail to let her precede him, she turned about in the saddle to find his bold gaze riveted to the curve of her buttocks, and she knew that he was as aware of her as she was of him.

As he called her attention to the newest calves following a single-file string of cows or a section of barbed-wire fence he had strung as a teenager, she could hear the pride in his voice. His uncompromising countenance even seemed more relaxed as he laughingly pointed out the first windmill in the territory. "My great-grandfather once tried to hang a cattle rustler from it, and his wife was so furious she held a rifle on her own husband and forced him to let the rascal go!"

Julie almost hated to return to the house, she was enjoying herself so much—and enjoying the way Nick looked at her and talked to her, the way a man would look and talk to a woman he cares about. But she reminded herself that Nick was very experienced with women. He knew all too well how to make each woman feel as if she were the only one he was interested in.

Still, her heart was thudding like a schoolgirl's by the time they returned to the barn. She knew she was destroying herself by loving Nick. Oh, she fully realized she could arouse his lust, but why couldn't she arouse his love? She forced her eyes to meet Nick's as he helped her dismount, his hands closing about her waist. Slowly, as if he were enjoying tormenting her, he slid her down along his length until her boots touched the barn's hay-covered floor.

His head bent over hers. "You're mine, Julie," he said huskily before his lips claimed hers in a punishing kiss. A flame of desire leaped to life in Julie, warming her with the want of Nick. She molded herself against his hard, lean body, setting fire to his blood as he had hers.

Her hands slid inside his jacket and up to his shoulders, savoring the heat that burned through his woolen shirt. Nick tipped her chin back, reclaiming her lips with a thorough kiss that left her shaken. Her Stetson slipped off, and her hair tumbled free about her shoulders.

The odor of the musty hay and old leather combined with Nick's own musky male scent to fill Julie with a kind of primeval abandon, so that when Nick finally released her with a shuddering reluctance and demanded roughly, "Tell me it isn't so—tell me you're not mine," she could only nod mutely and offer her lips up to the possessive mouth.

The warm hay was their bed, the nickering horses their watchguards, as Nick divested Julie of her jacket and Levi's and finally her sweater and underclothes. And what began in the rough heat of desire turned into a sweet passion of giving. When Nick withdrew from Julie, his body still partially covering hers, she closed her eyes, unable to meet his searching gaze. She was afraid she would find the look of indifference stamped on his face now that she had willingly given herself to him.

Nick reached up and disentangled a piece of hay from Julie's ruffled curls. "My grandmother's right, you know. You are an enchantress, Julie Raffer."

Julie's heart shriveled inside. Why couldn't he have said something about love? Suddenly the warmth that Nick's lovemaking had ignited flickered out, and the chill winter air seeped in around her nude body. She rolled from him and gathered up her clothes. He lay there, watching her, and a flush suffused her golden skin as she struggled into her jeans before his passionate gaze.

When the last of her jacket's buttons were

fastened, she turned on him. "You were right, Nick, I *am* yours. My body's yours—but never my heart!"

With the lie on her lips, she spun around and stalked to the house. As she entered the living room, Elizabeth, who was sitting in a rocker near the fire, looked up from a book she was reading. Julie knew then that Nick must have inherited his observant gaze from his grandmother, for the old woman took one look at Julie's flushed face and said, "I can see Nick's eloquence with words fails him when it comes to love."

"Love?" Julie echoed. Slowly she crossed to stand before the fire. She held her hands out to absorb the blazing fire's heat. "Mrs. Waggoner—Elizabeth—I can't continue to deceive you." She looked at the old woman and, embarrassed, returned her gaze to the orange-red flames. "Nick and I—we didn't marry for love. We were, I guess you might say, compromised."

Elizabeth made a chortling grunt. "Most people in my day didn't marry for love, either. But they came to love each other. As you and Nick have."

Julie turned now to fully face the woman. "It's true, Elizabeth, I've fallen in love with your grandson. But he doesn't love me."

The old woman put aside her book. "Don't let Nick's cool exterior fool you." She sighed and said, "As you must know by now, Nick loves San Ramon, but the years he spent here growing up were often marked by violent and bitter quarrels between my daughter and her husband—his parents.

"But, Julie, just as he loves this place and won't admit it, he loves you. Give my grandson time."

Chapter Ten

Below the Sangre de Cristos the capital of New Mexico sparkled like a diamond against the black velvet darkness of Christmas Eve. As the Blazer descended into Santa Fe, it passed homes that were gaily decorated with Christmas candles anchored in brown paper sacks called *luminarias*. It was supposed to be a time of joy to be spent with those you love; yet Julie, who was with the one man she loved, felt no joy as she watched the city's colorful lights pass by her window.

Throughout the return trip from San Ramon, she had kept her head averted from Nick's chiseled profile. The silence in the car had been unbearable for her. She had wanted

Nick to rage at her, to threaten her into submission, anything but his cool, dispassionate treatment of her.

It was as if he were confident she would eventually surrender totally to him and content to wait until she did. And Julie knew all too well Nick's unlimited patience. It was the patience of a hunter. She could only think how ironical it was that the thing she wanted to do most, surrender to Nick with both her body and her heart, would mean losing him.

Nick halted the Blazer before their darkened home, but when Julie moved to get out he said, "Wait. I have a surprise for you."

Julie tried to make out his expression in the blackness of the car, but it was unreadable. She let him lead her to the house and stood passively outside the doorway while he turned on the living-room lights. "All right," he said.

Slowly she walked inside. For a minute, unaccustomed to the bright lights, she did not notice anything. Her gaze moved around the room; she wondered what it was Nick wanted her to see. Then she saw it, above the fireplace.

Suspended from the gypsum-whitewashed wall was a gigantic blue sailfish, its streamlined body arched in flight, its spotted tail fanned wide. It was the sailfish she had caught in Cozumel!

"That's one of the reasons I wanted to go to San Ramon," Nick said quietly behind her. "I wanted to get you out of the house so the sailfish could be mounted in time for Christmas."

For someone else a mounted sailfish for Christmas might be a letdown, but for Julie it showed he had thought of their honeymoon and that one sunny afternoon when everything was right between them.

Julie turned around to face Nick, who leaned casually against the doorway, watching her reaction. She bit her lower lip, trying to contain the emotions that filled her. Joy, pleasure, surprise. "Nick, I . . ." She could not find the words, and he made no effort to help her.

Unable to restrain herself, Julie ran across the space that separated them and threw her arms about Nick's neck. Her lips brushed the warm hollow beneath his jaw, and she felt the muscle there flicker in response. "Nick," she breathed, "I lo—" But she caught back the betraying word in time and said, "I think it's the most wonderful gift anyone has ever given me."

Nick's hands went to her waist, and he set her from him. He looked down into her up-turned face. At last he said, "I wanted something special for you, because you are a very special person."

Julie wanted so badly to believe him. She wanted to believe that she *was* special to him. *Just for the Christmas holidays,* she told herself, *I will let myself believe Nick. I won't ask questions.* Shyly she pulled away. "I have something for you also, Nick."

She disappeared into the bedroom and returned with a small box wrapped in Christmas paper. "It seems we both had the same thing on our mind when we picked out gifts," she said softly as he unwrapped the box.

He took out the reel as reverently as if he were handling some great religious artifact. "You don't already have one, do you?" Julie asked anxiously.

Nick smiled then, and she was certain she saw pleasure in his eyes. "You won't believe it," he said, slipping his hand up around her neck in an intimate gesture that only a husband or a lover would use, "but I had a reel like this. It was my favorite, and I dropped it in Elephant Butte Lake. I've been meaning to try and find another one but just haven't had the chance."

He bent over her and gently brushed her lips with his. "Thank you, Julie," he whispered.

Reluctantly Julie stepped out of his embrace and began to gather up the discarded Christmas paper and wrapping. She was besieged by conflicting emotions. At one moment she wanted Nick to make love to her again, for her skin still burned with the ferocity of his lovemaking that afternoon. On the other hand, each time she gave herself up to Nick, she felt as if she were losing a part of herself. Soon she would be nothing but a mindless puppet in his control . . . and then she would become like the other women he had tired of so quickly. All except for Sheila Morrison, she reminded herself.

Nick solved her dilemma for her, for when she came out of the bathroom that evening dressed in a shimmering white lace and satin nightgown, the lights were out, and Nick, sprawled on his stomach on his side of the immense bed, seemed to be asleep. Julie lay between the cold sheets thinking how much better it must have been in Elizabeth's and her own grandmother's day when couples were forced to sleep together in much narrower beds, touching, feeling, hearing the soft breathing of their loved ones. She would willingly have bet that it was extremely difficult under those conditions to stay angry . . . or indifferent.

Yet she could hardly call Nick indifferent Christmas Day. If anything, he was attentive. He built a roaring fire in the fireplace and helped in the kitchen as Julie prepared the Christmas dinner. Once, as she bent over the open oven to test the duck she was roasting, Nick's hands encircled her waist to pull her back against him. Julie's head tipped backward on his shoulder. She was afraid to move, to break the spell, as Nick's teeth played gently with her ear and his hands ran slowly, tantalizingly, over her hips to press against the taut muscles of her abdomen.

"You know, Julie," he said lightly, "you tempt me to forgo that savory duck dinner in lieu of other delectable treats."

Julie twisted in his arms so that she was facing him. "And you tempt me, Nick," she said bravely. She met his searching gaze unflinchingly. "You know you've made me want you, even when I swore I didn't. You've won. Isn't that what you wanted from me?"

"It'll do for a start," Nick said and, taking the spatula from her hand, set it on the counter. He untied the bow of her apron, letting the apron flutter to the floor at their feet.

One by one his fingers loosed the buttons of her silk print blouse. When his hands slipped around her rib cage to free her breasts from her bra, Julie knew she was lost. By the time Nick made her his, she knew he would have no doubt of her love for him.

But I'll make certain your brain and body burn with the memory of our lovemaking, Nicholas Raffer, she silently vowed.

With deliberate leisureliness, she unbuttoned Nick's shirt. Nick's brows raised questioningly, as though to ask her if she understood the implications of what she was doing.

Her hand reached for the snap of his slacks, her fingers deftly loosening the catch. Still Nick did not move. His eyes scorched her face. Julie's fingers halted at the zipper, and she stood on tiptoe, her hands splaying against his chest for balance, and kissed the carved lines of his lips before playfully teasing them with her tongue.

"Dinner can wait," Nick growled. He reached behind her to switch off the oven, then gathered her up in his arms. Julie could hear Nick's heart thudding furiously in tempo with her own. When he went to lay her on the bed, she pulled him down with her. Tonight she would play the siren!

Her hands cupped the squared-off lines of his jaw, and she drew his lips down to hers. Nick's tongue explored her mouth with a thoroughness that left her yearning for more when his lips at last deserted hers to travel down the smooth column of her neck.

Her fingers entwined in his hair as his lips flicked the hard buttons of her breasts. "The morsels you offer are much more tempting than the roast duck," he whispered against the soft mound.

The realization slowly dawned on Julie that no longer was she the seducer. Nick had swiftly turned the tables, and it was she who lay trembling, waiting for him to make her complete. He came to her then, gently, tenderly, patiently. And when it was over, she buried her head in the hollow of his shoulder, so he would not see the ecstasy, the love, that she felt surely must shine in her eyes.

"Sleepy?" Nick asked, nuzzling her temple with his chin.

Julie shook her head, afraid even to speak. She wanted the intimate, loving feeling between them to continue, to flow like a river out of their lovemaking into every corner of their lives, the way the love her parents shared completely filled their lives.

But the ringing of the telephone shattered the brief, ecstatic moment, and Nick cursed beneath his breath. He raised on one elbow and looked at Julie with a grin. "If it's that Dee Morley, I swear I'll get a bill passed to prohibit gossip columnists from using telephones."

"Should we just let it ring?" Julie asked uncertainly.

Nick sighed and unwillingly withdrew his gaze from the sight of Julie's high, firm breasts. "No," he said, rising from the bed; "it must be something important for whoever it is to call on Christmas Day."

Julie's eyes followed his lean, muscle-corded body across the shadowy room. Her own body felt bereft now that he had left her, and she mentally cursed the telephone herself.

Nick turned to her, his eyes hard as stones, and held out the receiver, saying, "It's for you." Julie looked from the receiver back to him, and he added harshly, "It's Jim Miller."

She gathered the rumpled sheet about her

and crossed to Nick, taking the receiver. "Hello?"

"Julie," Jim said, "I hate to disturb you, but I wanted to catch you before you took off for somewhere, and I was unable to reach you yesterday. We're going to have to do a New Year's special edition on 'New Mexico—Its Wealth and Its Waste.' Do you think you could come in for a couple of days and work up a piece for me on the state's political issues?"

Julie looked to Nick, who was calmly shrugging into his knit shirt. Perhaps she had mistaken the anger she had seen on his face for irritation. "Of course, Jim, I'd love to."

"Great! I'll fill you in on the slant I want you to take tomorrow."

Julie hung up the receiver. She hoped Nick would question her about the call so she could explain to him about Jim, but he showed no curiosity at all. "Nick," she began hesitantly, "Jim wants me to do some articles for the *Sun*. It's a rush job, or he wouldn't have bothered—"

"Fine," Nick said evenly. He kissed her briefly on the forehead and said, "Let's eat. I've got a lot of paperwork to catch up on."

Whatever intimacy Julie had hoped to establish was gone, and Nick returned to the cool, detached man who had rescued her and taken her to his mountain cabin. If he resented the hours she spent working late with Jim, he did not show it. In fact, he seemed to stay as busy as she.

She often feared that someone else had taken her place in Nick's arms, for he did not seek her out at all now. She half expected him to tell her he was ready to put an end to their marriage and wondered if her empty threat to get even with him through her column kept him from it.

Yet somehow she didn't think her threat would stop Nick if he decided to end their mockery of a marriage. And then there was the fact that she occasionally had caught his lazy gaze on her as she moved about the house—which gave her hope that she still might have the power to arouse his interest.

Late one night that same week she awoke to the blustery roar of one of winter's northers that would sometimes descend on Santa Fe with sudden and rapid violence. Julie lay huddled on her side of the bed, unable to sleep and wishing fervently for the warm comfort of Nick's arms.

The winter storm must have awakened him also, for a few minutes later she heard him shift and saw the flare of a match. She said nothing, but when he ground out the cigarette stub, he turned to her and drew her into his arms, pressing her head against his shoulder. "Try and get some sleep, love," he said. "The storm will soon pass by."

She fell asleep, cradled in Nick's arms, with

hope in her heart . . . a hope that was dashed the next day when Nick told her of the invitation they had to attend a special exhibition of one of New Mexico's Indian artists that Sheila Morrison was sponsoring.

Julie paused in brushing her hair. She looked in the mirror at Nick's reflection. "Do we have to go?" she asked, forcing a lightness to her voice. "I really don't know that much about art."

"It'd be a good chance to learn," Nick said, loosening the knot in his tie. "Besides, part of my platform when I ran for senator was to support Indian involvement in our state, and I feel it's my duty to attend the function."

Julie tried to tell herself she was making something out of nothing . . . that until Nick came to her and told her he no longer wanted her as his wife, she had a chance to make him love her.

Still, it was with a sense of foreboding that she prepared for the exhibition Saturday afternoon. She donned a toast-colored crepe skirt with a matching blouse that frothed about the neck and wrists. She studied her face in the mirror as she applied a faint touch of blusher and decided she looked very attractive. But was she attractive enough to compete with Sheila's stunning beauty? she wondered dismally.

She dreaded so much another confrontation with the beautiful, sophisticated woman that she was hardly aware of the drive along Santa Fe's historical streets. And when Nick stopped the car in the ancient plaza for a tourist who was photographing the *Palacio*, the oldest public building in the United States, she almost pleaded a headache so that she might forgo the dreaded meeting with Sheila.

The exhibition was being held at a gallery located on the winding, tree-shaded Canyon Road where fine old adobe homes rubbed elbows with art studios and quaint restaurants. A little bell tinkled when Nick opened the door of the two-story art gallery. Although they were early, there were already half a dozen people viewing the artist's paintings or milling around the elaborately decorated table set with a punch bowl, champagne glasses, and dishes of cheese wedges.

To Julie's relief Sheila was nowhere in sight, and she could only hope Nick would not want to stay long. As usual, Nick knew several of the people there and was introducing Julie to an older couple who shared an opera box next to his when Julie saw Sheila descending the stairs. With her was the Indian artist, Paul Htchapi.

The short young Indian, who wore a red flannel band around his long hair and a khaki shirt with military trousers, should have been the center of attention, since it was his paintings that were being exhibited. But it was

Sheila who caught everyone's admiring gaze. She had swept her tawny mane atop her head in an elegant knot, and the blue-green chiffon designer's dress, which matched her eyes, swirled about her lovely long legs. Julie estimated the dress had to have cost the woman a tidy sum.

She felt Nick's hand at her elbow as Sheila, with Paul at her side, moved across the room toward them. "I was so glad you could come this afternoon," Sheila said, taking Nick's arm. Her hungry gaze caressed Nick's spare, sun-browned face. "Your presence here, Nick, will do a lot to support your upcoming campaign."

For the first time Sheila looked at Julie. "Have you two had any champagne yet? Paul, do be a doll and get Julie a glass while I talk to Nick about his campaign."

Helplessly Julie let Paul propel her toward the punch table as Sheila possessively took Nick's arm and led him away. "Are you interested more in my abstracts—or maybe one of my portraits, Mrs. Raffer?" Paul was asking, and Julie forced her attention back to the young Indian.

She hardly tasted the champagne he handed her and only half listened as he pointed out some of his favorite paintings. The downstairs lobby was rapidly filling, and she was beginning to feel lost. She knew none of the people, and, to make matters worse, Paul was starting to make calf eyes at her.

Where was Nick? And Sheila?

Quietly Julie excused herself from Paul's smitten attention. She really was developing the headache she had almost feigned earlier. She didn't know if it was the champagne she had drunk or an empty stomach or just the sight of seeing Sheila with Nick that made her head throb so, but she was ready to go home.

She made her way through the press of people, looking for Nick, but he was nowhere on the lower floor. The second floor, which contained an array of paintings not currently on exhibition, was darkened and deserted, and Julie had almost turned back to the staircase when she saw a light from a room toward the rear of the gallery floor. It was with a sick feeling in her stomach that she made her way toward the light. She wanted to turn back, afraid of what she might find, but her footsteps took her ever nearer.

The door was partially open, and Julie had nearly knocked when she heard Sheila's sultry voice. "With me at your side, Nick, the governor's mansion is ours. But that little country hick of yours will only stand in your way. Oh, darling, I can't imagine whatever made you want to marry her!"

There was a silence that hurt Julie worse

than Sheila's words ever could have, for she could only too well imagine Nick holding Sheila in his arms at that moment, his mouth bruising Sheila's in a passionate kiss. Then Nick's voice, husky with laughter, broke the long silence. "Let me tell you about my little country hick, Sheila . . ."

But Julie did not wait to hear. The pain in her heart was great enough as it was. She fled down the stairs and pushed herself through the crowd in the lobby. Outside, she leaned against the pink stucco building and gulped great quantities of air, trying to choke back the sobs that rose to her throat.

Why had she not admitted sooner that Sheila and Nick were made for each other? As Sheila had pointed out, she would only stand in the way of Nick's rising political career. But, dear God, she loved him so much! It would be so hard to give him up!

A young couple getting out of a cab looked at her strangely as they entered the gallery, and Julie knew she must be making a spectacle of herself with the tears streaming down her face. Quickly she hailed the vacated cab, wanting only to get away, to run from Nick and Sheila's mocking laughter.

"Where to, miss?" the cabbie asked.

Where, indeed? Where could she go? What would she do? She knew she could no longer stay in the same vicinity as Nick. It would be too heart-wrenching to see his name in the newspapers, to hear it on the radio, and to see his wickedly handsome face on the television.

She would see his face often enough the rest of her life in her dreams. Every waking hour would be filled with thoughts of Nicholas Raffer.

Chapter Eleven

Julie laid her forehead on the top of the typewriter and took deep breaths. Soon, she told herself, the nausea would pass. Her fingers trembled so much that she had hit all the wrong keys. And one finger was bare of a wedding ring.

Her mother came into the bedroom. "Julie, are you feeling all right?"

Julie looked up at her mother's concerned face, which was finely sculptured like her own but framed by short, stylishly cut brown hair streaked with gray. She managed a smile. "I guess I'm just tired, Mom. I stayed up late last night, trying to finish the third chapter of the book."

Mary Dever's brows knitted in worry. "Are you sure that's it?" She crossed over to the desk and sat on Julie's bed across from it. "You haven't been yourself, Julie. Since you came home six weeks ago you've been walking around the house like someone who's been told she has only a month to live."

Julie had to smile, though she indeed felt as if she had died six weeks before. She had returned home—Nick's home, she reminded herself—half in fear of Nick's returning before she could pack her suitcases. Within half an hour she had quickly loaded the few belongings she possessed in her station wagon.

It had been difficult to drive away without a backward glance, without hoping that Nick would suddenly materialize and order her to stop. But she had done it; she had driven straight through to Little Elm, Texas, a nineteen-hour trip.

"No, Mom, I'm not dying," she reassured her mother.

Mrs. Dever put out her hand to touch Julie's. "Honey, whatever argument you and Nick had can't be as terrible as all that. The love you two have can bridge anything."

Julie looked out her second-story bedroom window. A late February snow blanketed the lawns outside and decorated the trees that were as barren of leaves as Julie's heart was barren of hope. She knew she would have to tell her parents sometime. They deserved that much.

Julie's gaze moved back to her mother's face, with its fine lines of age about the eyes put there by years of joy, sorrow, disappointment, and laugher. "Mom, Nick—when he married me, well . . . he didn't really . . ." She sighed. "I guess I had better begin again. It starts with an accident I had last year."

A faint smile touched her mother's lips. "And Nick rescued you?"

Julie gave her mother a suspicious glance, but the woman's soft face wore a serene, patient look. Encouraged, Julie proceeded to tell her mother the entire story, holding nothing back. "So you see, Mom," she finished, "Nick married me to save my honor. And his," she added bitterly.

After a moment her mother said, "Do you really think that Nicholas married you to keep you from writing any further disparaging articles? I'm sure that as a politician in the public eye he has faced scurrilous attacks before and will again, no doubt."

"You don't understand Nicholas Raffer. He'd stop at nothing to have his way." Julie sighed again. "But it makes no difference. We hated each other before we ever met. And now—now he thinks I'm interested in another man."

"And are you?"

"Of course not! There could never be anyone but . . ."

"Then you're in love with Nicholas Raffer,
aren't you?"

Julie rested her head on the typewriter
again. She had never felt so miserable in all
her life. "Yes," she admitted at last. "I love
him. But I'm not right for him, Mom," she
whispered. "There's another woman."

"Oh?" Julie thought her mother would be
shocked, but she merely said, "Do you know
that he has been seeing her since your marriage?"

"Well, no—not exactly."

"Has he told you that you're not right for
him?"

Julie raised her head. "No—but, Mom, I
have my pride. I wasn't going to wait around
for him to tell me to leave."

"Pride—such a foolish thing for God to give
us humans! I don't suppose you've told Nicholas how you feel? I think you owe it to him,
Julie. He not only helped you out of the
accident and took care of you afterward, he
married you. You owe it to him to tell him you
love him."

The memory of him dancing with Sheila
came back to Julie, her vision of how perfect
they had looked together, and she said abruptly, "Never!"

"And your marriage? At some point—if you

don't intend to return to Nicholas—you've got to communicate to him your intentions of ending it."

"I know." Julie rose from her chair and began pacing her bedroom. "I know I've got to do it, and I don't know why I'm waiting. I ought to get it over with . . . but I can't, not right now. It's too soon. Perhaps within another month I'll have the courage, Mom."

Her mother stood up and went to the door. "I think you ought to listen to your heart. It may be warning you that this marriage shouldn't be ended at all."

"This marriage should never have taken place to begin with," Julie said listlessly as she stood at the window looking out on the winter wasteland. Was the high desert in New Mexico covered with snow at that moment?

Julie's grandmother was more voluble than Mrs. Dever on the subject of Julie's shattered marriage. "Poppycock! What a lot of rot, as I've heard you young'ns say often enough!" The old woman never missed a stitch on the sweater she was knitting as she rocked before the roaring fire in the living room's hearth. "I gave you more credit, child, than being one of those pups that tuck their tails and run. You gonna let that hussy have your husband without a fight?"

At times Julie was fighting mad. She told

herself she was a fool to have given up Nick without a fight. Even if she could never make him love her, she would have had what most women dream of—a handsome, successful, and famous husband. What difference if he did not love her? She could console herself with her husband's substantial checking account.

But Julie knew she was a fool. She wanted Nick's love, not his money. And though she might have fought for that love, she could not bring herself to stand in the way of his becoming governor. She loved him too much to hold him back.

Julie worked the rest of that month and on through March on her novel. She told herself that she was happy, that she was doing something she had always wanted to do, write a book. But she was not happy, and she felt sick all the time.

Her mother tried to get her to go out with old friends, and her father tried to persuade her to go fishing with him. "The bass are really biting good right now," he coaxed her. But Julie preferred to remain alone.

"You have to get out of the house, Julie!" her mother told her one afternoon when the northwesterly winter winds had let up and the sun peeked through the gray clouds.

For once Julie agreed with her mother. Surprised at Julie's capitulation, her mother said, "Wonderful! Perhaps you'd like to do some shopping. We could drive in to Dallas, have lunch in the Zodiac Room at Neiman's, then spend the afternoon—"

"Mom," Julie said, not knowing exactly how to begin, "I'd like to go into town by myself."

Her mother cast her a quizzical look but did not appear to be hurt by Julie's rejection of her suggestion. "All right, darling. I'm just relieved you're getting out. Try to forget about everything for a while and have a good time."

Having a good time was not on Julie's mind as she made the hour-long trip into Dallas. Only one thing occupied her mind that day, and the doctor confirmed her suspicion after she had waited another hour to get in to see him.

"I'd say around the middle of September, Mrs. Raffer," he told her as he polished his thick glasses. "As narrow as you are through the pelvis, we'll want to keep a close check on your pregnancy during the last few weeks. But I don't really anticipate any problem, since you're in excellent health."

"I see," Julie said tonelessly. But she really did not see. She really could not understand how it could have happened to her. She could count the number of times Nick had made love to her on one hand . . . and she had had to conceive!

She did not remember the drive back to Little Elm that afternoon. She did not recall how she got there, but for almost an hour she sat out in front of Hickory Creek at her father's favorite fishing spot. Great willow and hickory trees arched over the creek, which was high with the melting of the snow. A squirrel, returning from some winter foray, scurried up a live oak denuded of leaves, and a cottontail bounded into the underbrush that edged the creek.

But Julie noticed none of this. She felt as if she were caught up in one of Texas's terrible tornadoes, whirled in the vortex until she was dizzy with the strain of her dilemma.

She could not continue to live off her parents. She was a grown woman . . . more than that, she was a mother-to-be. She had the baby to think about now.

She would have to get a job. Secretarial positions paid good salaries in Dallas. And she needed to find an apartment. She thought of her novel and knew it would have to wait. She had responsibilities now.

The chill that was creeping into the car reminded her that the afternoon was getting later and she should be returning to her parents' home. She would have to tell them they would soon be grandparents—and Granny would be a great-grandmother. What would the irascible old woman have to say about that? Julie wondered.

The old woman laid her napkin beside her dinner plate and chuckled. "That Nicholas Raffer didn't waste any time, did he!"

Julie's mother rolled her eyes at the old woman's candor but had to laugh. "That's wonderful, Julie!" she said when she had regained her breath. Now her eyes watched Julie carefully, trying to gauge her daughter's reaction to the news.

Julie's father set down his glass of tea. "It'll take some time getting used to the idea," he said slowly. "It seems like only yesterday you were tagging after me on the river bank." He smiled tenderly at her. "How about making it another girl just like you?"

Julie had to laugh. "I'm afraid I have nothing to do with that, Dad. The father determines . . ." She broke off, unable to finish.

"Julie," her mother said, "we love you and want only your happiness. But don't you think Nicholas has a right to know about the child—after all, he's just as much the parent of the baby as you are. You're being unfair to him."

Tears stung Julie's eyes. "I don't know what's the matter with me," she whispered. "I seem to be so weepy all the time now."

"I know what's wrong with you," her mother said gently. "You're pregnant. Julie, you're welcome to stay here as long as you want. But this is a special time you should be sharing with the baby's father. Put aside your pride and go back to him."

Julie wadded up her napkin. "Mom, I can't! Now more than ever. I wouldn't want him to take me back just because I'm carrying his child!"

"It's all right, Julie," her father said, seeing that the mere talk of Nick upset his daughter. "We won't interfere, I promise. We'll abide by whatever decision you choose to make."

Julie put off hunting for an apartment until she had found a job and received her first paycheck. Realizing that most employers would not want to hire a woman who would soon be taking off to have a baby, she decided to take a job with one of the temporary employment agencies until after the baby was old enough for her to go back to work full time.

Sometimes she would look in the mirror at her concave stomach, and it was difficult for her to believe she actually carried a child inside her . . . if it were not for the persistent nausea and the memory of the nights of love that she had spent in Nick's arms.

Julie tried not to let herself wonder what woman was in his arms now, but she kept seeing Sheila Morrison's haughty face looking seductively into Nick's blazing blue eyes.

That first week that Julie worked seemed like the worst in her life—with the exception of the week she had left Nick. The first three days she worked for a small insurance company whose secretary was on vacation. And the last two days she replaced an oil firm's secretary who had eloped and not returned to work.

She did not know which was worse—repulsing the passes made by her boss, who had no idea he was flirting with a mother-to-be, or choking back the nausea that threatened to rise in her throat throughout the day.

The pills the doctor had given her did not seem to be helping to relieve the nausea very much, and every day she wondered if she would have enough energy to fight the heavy Dallas traffic and make the long drive back to Little Elm.

It was during one of those long drives back that Julie castigated herself. She had to be the world's biggest fool. To be married to a senator and carrying his child . . . she could have anything she wanted. If not from him, then from the law courts. No more drudgery in Cement City, and she thought of the beautiful, cozy home out on the high scenic desert of New Mexico.

And she thought of Nick—the man, not the senator—and her pulses began to race with the old desire that her love for him inflamed in her heart.

She was a fool seven times over—and she would probably be a fool the rest of her life, but she would not force herself on a man who did not love her.

At least spring would soon arrive, she thought as her gaze noted the hint of green creeping into the brown yards that bordered the street where her parents lived. Surely her spirits would liven up with the arrival of beautiful weather.

As she approached her parents' home, she slowed her car, noting the strange automobile parked at the curb. Then her heart lurched with the realization the car was Nick's Blazer!

Julie turned into the driveway and switched off her car's ignition. She sat behind the steering wheel, shaking. Had Nick tracked her down because she had brought disgrace on his head when she deserted him . . . or, worse, had he come because her parents had summoned him?

She laid her forehead against the steering wheel, wishing with all her soul that she did not have to go inside and face Nick Raffer. What a formidable opponent! But she knew that sooner or later the matter of their divorce would have to be settled, and at least now it would be done on her home ground.

She looked in the rearview mirror. Her green eyes sparkled with the challenge. In fact, her whole body positively radiated. Her mother had told her that the special beauty came with the bloom of pregnancy. She ran her fingers through her luxuriant dark hair, which seemed to be even silkier, and unbuttoned the top two buttons of the rust-colored linen sheath dress she wore so that the cleavage of her breasts, ripening with pregnancy, was visible. She wondered why she was going to all this trouble, but told herself she would feel better prepared to battle the more confidence she had in herself.

As she walked up the sidewalk to the veranda, her knees were trembling so badly she thought she was going to either have to remove the high heels she wore or fall flat on her face. To make matters worse, the doorknob would not even turn, so slippery was her hand with nervous perspiration.

The door gave and Nick stood there—his dark face just as self-contained as ever, so that Julie could not tell what kind of furious thoughts might be running through his mind. She looked past him, but the living room was vacant, denying her the support of her parents or grandmother. From the kitchen came the sounds of her mother preparing dinner.

Julie's gaze came back to Nick's penetrating blue eyes. She wanted to make her feet move, but they would not, and she had to clutch the door to steady herself. "Nick," she breathed. "It's nice to see you." Where had all the air gone? Was that why her voice sounded so strange to her ears?

"Is it?" Nick asked, and Julie knew that if she had the strength she would have turned and run from those mocking eyes. But Nick did not even give her the chance. He took her elbow. "Please come in—it *is* your house . . . or your *parents',*" he said pointedly.

His touch weakened her even further, and she withdrew her elbow as soon as it was politely possible and crossed to the rocking chair. "Please sit down," she said, trying to muster a calmness she did not feel.

Nick did not take a seat in the easy chair she had indicated but remained standing, his thumbs hooked in the belt loops of his jeans. Except for the smoothly shaven jaw he looked much the same as the first time they had met. "I suppose you're here to discuss our divorce," Julie said and rushed on. "I had planned to see a lawyer as soon as I received my first pay—"

Nick's hand caught her arms and jerked her to her feet. "Hell, no, I'm not here to discuss our divorce! I'd like to throttle you right now, but I'm taking you back to Santa Fe with me, Julie Raffer. Your home's there, not living with your parents!"

"I suppose my parents called you?" she asked, fearing he knew her secret.

Nick's dark brows met over the bridge of his

nose in an expression of confusion. "No, they didn't. It would have helped if they had. You can't imagine what you've put me through, not to mention the trouble it took to track you down!"

Julie pulled away from the wrath on Nick's face. "I—then why do you want me to go back with you? I don't understand. There's no longer any reason to protect my virtue," she said caustically. "And now that I'm not there to cause you any trouble, you're free to divorce me and—and marry her . . . Sheila."

Julie was having trouble keeping the anguish out of her voice. Just the sight of Nick, so tall and ruggedly handsome, his presence dominating the room, was enough to make her lose the tight hold she was keeping on her self-control. Another second of looking at those piercing, all-consuming eyes and she would throw herself in his arms and rain kisses on that beloved face.

"Sheila? What has all this to do with Sheila?"

Julie's brows raised in surprise. "I thought—Don't you want to marry Sheila?"

Nick caught Julie in his arms again, crushing her against his chest. His hand cupped her chin, forcing her to raise her eyes to meet his. "Julie," he said huskily, "you must believe me . . . there's never been any other woman on my mind—or in my heart—since the night I pulled you from your overturned car. With your wily leprechaun face, you've possessed me, so I could think of nothing else but you!"

"Me?" Julie asked, not really believing she was hearing Nick correctly.

At last the mockery left Nick's lips. "Yes, you," he said tenderly. "Your courage in the face of the accident, your spirit in spite of your pain . . . they commanded my admiration. And later your womanly body . . . in my cabin . . . with that wonderfully childlike virtue . . . the combination was something I had never run up against in all my affairs with other women."

"But . . . but you and Sheila are so well suited. I'm just a coun—"

Nick's impatient kiss silenced Julie's confused protest, and she gave herself up to the flame of passion that only Nick could ignite. His mouth crushed hers as if he could not get enough of her. At last, when Julie felt as though molten lava surely poured through her feverish body, Nick released her.

"Don't you see, Julie," he said with a tender smile, "we were made for each other . . . from our love of the outdoors to politics, even though we don't always agree. That's what makes knowing each other interesting."

"But I thought you didn't like me," Julie said, reveling in the exquisite feeling of his strong arms about her waist.

"And I thought you hated me. So there

seemed no other way to court you but to pressure you into marriage. Dee's call gave me the opportunity . . . which I sorely regretted for so long afterward."

Julie's breath caught deep in her lungs, still fearful that this might be a scheme of Nick's retaliation. "Why?"

"Because being married to you—and not being able to have you—was worse than any kind of torture the Indians could have devised. And to see you in Jim's arms the night of the governor's ball and later him holding your hand in the restaurant—at that moment I would have gladly killed him and gone to prison for the rest of my life. Then, when you began to spend so much time with him on that project, I almost gave up hope of your ever coming to love me."

Julie's hand slipped up to caress Nick's square-cut jaw. "But, darling, I tried to tell you that Jim meant nothing to me."

"I know that now. But for the longest time after you left I thought you had gone to him. I told myself you deserved the opportunity to be happy with Jim. I read the *Sun* every day, searching for your byline. When none of your scathing articles appeared blasting me, and later when no divorce papers came, I began to get suspicious.

"I called the newspaper, and the personnel department told me you had left—with no forwarding address. Let me tell you, love, even with the information resources I have, it was hard trying to trace you down. I remembered you telling me in Cozumel you lived somewhere in Texas, but I couldn't recall where. Then I remembered your friend Pam, and I thought if anyone might know she would."

Julie's eyebrows arched in surprise. "I made Pam swear not to tell anyone where I went!"

Nick smiled. "She was reluctant at first. But I managed to persuade her of my sincere intentions of good will toward you. She finally gave me your parents' address."

His hands came up to catch either side of Julie's temples, his fingers winding themselves in her long hair. "Julie, tell me that you love me, also," he commanded. "Put me out of this misery."

Julie stood on tiptoe, her arms sliding up to encircle Nick's neck. "Oh, Nick, I've loved you since that first night you so thoughtfully took off my tennis shoes." She kissed his lips lightly and said, "Shall I tell you more?"

"Tell me everything that comes into that delightfully provocative mind of yours. If you had told me you loved me to begin with it would have saved us a lot of trouble."

"Shall I tell you that you need to add another bedroom to our home?"

"I'll be damned if I will! You're sleeping in my bed where you belong!" His head bent to claim another kiss, but Julie dodged the demanding lips. "But, Nick, the bedroom's not for me," she said with a teasing smile. "It's for the baby we're expecting in September."

She saw the surprise that froze Nick, and for a moment she feared he would not want her if she was with child. Then he swept her up in his arms. "Julie! It's true?" he asked. "I'm going to be a father?"

And at her timid nod, he whispered, "I can't believe it! An hour ago I thought my life, without you, never looked darker. And now I've not only your love—but someone else to love, too!"

Then the aloof senator from New Mexico astounded Julie by shouting, "I'm going to be a father!"

Julie's father stuck his head through the doorway. "Just make sure if it's a girl, Nick, you'll teach her how to fish and hunt!"

Silhouette Romance

THE NEW NAME IN LOVE STORIES

Six new titles every month bring you the best in romance.
Set all over the world, exciting and brand new stories about
people falling in love:

Silhouette Romance

SILHOUETTE ROMANCE

THE NEW NAME IN LOVE STORIES

SILHOUETTE ROMANCE

THE NEW NAME IN LOVE STORIES

Silhouette Romance

EXCITING MEN,
EXCITING PLACES, HAPPY ENDINGS . . .

Contemporary romances for today's women

If there's room in your life for a little more romance,
SILHOUETTE ROMANCES are for you.

And you won't want to miss a single one so start
your collection now.

Each month, six very special love stories will be yours
from SILHOUETTE.

Look for them wherever books are sold
or order from the coupon below.

*All these books are available at your local bookshop or
newsagent, or can be ordered direct from the publisher. Just
tick the titles you want and fill in the form below.*

Prices and availability subject to change without notice.

SILHOUETTE BOOKS, P.O. Box 11, Falmouth, Cornwall.
Please send cheque or postal order, and allow the following for
postage and packing:

U.K. — 40p for one book, plus 18p for the second book, and
13p for each additional book ordered, up to £1.49 maximum.

B.F.P.O. and EIRE — 40p for the first book, 18p for the
second book, and 13p per copy for the next 7 books, 7p per
book thereafter.

OTHER OVERSEAS CUSTOMERS — 60p for the first book
plus 18p per copy for each additional book.

Name ....

Address..

....